The Hex Girls

A ROGUE THORN

A ROGUE THORN

LILY MEADE

Random House 🏠 New York

Random House Books for Young Readers
An imprint of Random House Children's Books
A division of Penguin Random House LLC
1745 Broadway, New York, NY 10019
penguinrandomhouse.com
GetUnderlined.com

Jacket art by Dario Brizuela

 Copyright © 2025 Hanna-Barbera.
SCOOBY-DOO and all related characters and elements
© &™ Hanna-Barbera. WB SHIELD: © &™ WBEI. (s25)

Penguin Random House values and supports copyright. Copyright fuels creativity, encourages diverse voices, promotes free speech, and creates a vibrant culture. Thank you for buying an authorized edition of this book and for complying with copyright laws by not reproducing, scanning, or distributing any part of it in any form without permission. You are supporting writers and allowing Penguin Random House to continue to publish books for every reader. Please note that no part of this book may be used or reproduced in any manner for the purpose of training artificial intelligence technologies or systems.

Random House and the colophon are registered trademarks of Penguin Random House LLC.

ISBN 978-0-593-81462-8 (trade)— ISBN 978-0-593-81463-5 (lib. bdg.)
ISBN 978-0-593-81464-2 (ebook)

Manufactured in the United States of America
1st Printing

The authorized representative in the EU for product safety and compliance is Penguin Random House Ireland, Morrison Chambers, 32 Nassau Street, Dublin D02 YH68, Ireland, https://eu-contact.penguin.ie.

Random House Children's Books supports the First Amendment and celebrates the right to read.

*For Padfoot and Colbie. Scooby made me a dog person,
but you made me a dog mom. You are the goodest girls.
I love you.*

PROLOGUE

I will not let her die for me.

The moonlight slices through the windows as I race ahead, trying to forget the others I'm leaving behind. They wouldn't want me to stop to help them. They chose this. *We* chose this.

We came here because of her.

If I'd known a year ago where befriending Mystery Inc. would lead me, I might have left Oakhaven the day they arrived. Maybe I wouldn't have waited until it was too late, until my life there was destroyed. Maybe I wouldn't have come here, to their hometown, and started down this miserable, ill-fated path.

If I could have ignored true magic, knowing the cost, maybe I would have done it. I would have stayed in a world where monsters were laughable, where the morbid and macabre lived only in my wardrobe.

If someone or something had warned me, maybe I would've run *from* her. Not *to* her.

But now, I wouldn't choose to go back to my life before— to a town where I was beloved instead of betrayed, to untested friendships with no fractures, to a time before I witnessed someone die right in front of me.

I would never go back. I could never give up what I have now. The kindness. The friendship.

Meeting Velma—trusting her—set fire to my life. Literally.

Her smile. Her laugh. Her intelligence. The specific way she says "jinkies."

Her belief in me, even when I gave her every reason to doubt. It's impossible. That case is closed. It's too late for me.

Hopefully I'm not too late for her.

CHAPTER ONE

I can't live here.

I blink rapidly as I scan the maze of boxes my father has already unloaded into what is supposed to be my new room, but it doesn't change the sight in front of me. "You're joking, right?" I ask him as I place Eldritch, my pet Venus flytrap, on the windowsill.

"It's the biggest room in the house," he says, as if that negates the horror of the color.

It's *pink*.

I spin on my heel to plead with him, gesturing widely to my . . . entire existence, really. I run my hands through the red streaks in my black hair, unfurling the travel bun I wore on the road trip here. Dad saw the house in listing photos before we got here, but I should have pressed him harder to give me a peek. I was just so grateful he agreed to let us move to Coolsville at all.

I don't know if I've ever seen such a nauseating pastel. He's right that the room itself is big. I'll have more than enough space. And the large window allows a lot of light into the room, but that only intensifies the suffocating glow of the Pepto-Bismol–colored paint. "Daddy," I say. "Come on."

"The family that lived here before us had twin toddlers," he confesses. "Three guesses as to what their gender was," he adds, smiling at his awful joke. His grin always takes up the entirety of his thin face, creasing his dark eyes. His mirth falters when I don't laugh, and he reaches out a hand to me and guides me toward a door opposite the one we came in.

He opens it. "It's also the only bedroom with a bathroom," he says. I peek my head inside this consolation prize. The matching decor mercifully ends at the cartoonish flowers painted on the door. The bathroom itself is an inoffensive white. It's small, but includes a shower and a sink with plenty of counter space.

"Can we paint it?" I ask desperately.

His thin grin fades further. "Maybe," he says. "In a few weeks, after I get my first couple of paychecks from the pharmacy, perhaps. I'll have to catch up on the moving expenses first."

I shoulder past him back into the pink dungeon. "Right," I say without turning around. "Of course." I drop to my knees in front of a box near the window, picking at the tape with a fingernail painted blood-red.

"We'll catch up," he says. "I promise. Selling my drugstore and the house in Oakhaven covered most of it, but we—"

"I get it," I say. "It's fine."

"Sally," he starts.

I finally get a grip on the tape and loudly rip it off to silence him. "I have a lot of unpacking to do," I say. I don't turn around to check, but from the silence on the hardwood floor, I sense he hasn't left yet. I feel his hand lightly brush the back of my head and resist the urge to duck forward to deny him even that. I asked for this fresh start, but I still can't forget why we had to leave Oakhaven in the first place.

My finger traces the block letters spelling *Thorn* over every crossed-out *Sally's Room* label Dad put on the moving boxes.

"I'll order some pizza in a bit," he says as his footsteps fade away. "I'll let you know when it's here."

"Thanks," I say quietly, even though I know he's too far away now to hear me.

I know he'd like me to give our relationship the same clean slate the rest of the move is granting us, but I can't forgive him. Not yet. He lied to me. He lied to the *entire town*. For money, of all things. And when things got bad, instead of coming forward on his own, a group of kids had to unmask him.

Oakhaven's being the hometown of horror novelist Ben Ravencroft wasn't enough for Dad and the mayor. They had to convince tourists that the town was haunted by the ghost of Ben's ancestor Sarah, a supposedly evil witch. I should've questioned it more, but the shift in the town's tourist attractions from colonial reenactments to supernatural tours made my band, the Hex Girls, a much more fitting option to headline the Harvest Festival.

That only made us look even guiltier when everything fell apart.

I rub the tape residue from my finger onto the cardboard and open my first box, fighting the urge to immediately close it again. There's nothing but framed pictures of everything and everyone I've left behind. I pick up the most recent: a photo of my band at the performance we almost didn't get to play. I wouldn't have chosen to frame this one, not with the singed trees still visible in the background, but it was a gift from the photographer herself.

Velma Dinkley. She and her friends were the ones who exposed my father. That would have been bad enough, but it turned out there was truth in my father's schemes. Sarah wasn't a Wiccan like me, falsely accused of dark magic. She truly was evil, and Ben Ravencroft had known it all along. He invited Velma and her friends to visit Oakhaven to help find her old spell book—not to exonerate Sarah, like he originally said, but to summon her spirit and spread their dark power together.

They almost succeeded. The Hex Girls and Mystery Inc. teamed up and stopped Ben and Sarah, but the damage to the town and our reputation was irreversible.

I stand up and check on Eldritch, placing the framed photo next to him to remind me why we had to come here. A cross-country move is rough on anyone, let alone a carnivorous plant whose first instinct upon disturbance is to close its traps and start digesting itself. Only one of his open traps seem to have closed prematurely, but I open the window anyway, hoping the hideous glow of my room tricks some bugs into thinking it's made of candy. "We'll get through this, Eldritch," I promise, more to myself than to him.

CHAPTER TWO

The people of Coolsville are just as colorful as my new room. I watch them meander on the streets below, in shades as varied as the leaves just beginning to change on the early-fall trees. I expected more palm trees when we moved to California. I haven't seen much of the town yet, but aside from the architecture and weather it's not that different from Oakhaven. They both take pride in being old-growth historic small towns, though Coolsville has clearly succeeded past relying solely on its gold rush period for tourism.

That was a factor when Luna, Dusk, and I were narrowing down where to relocate. I didn't want to move someplace where too many questions would be asked of the new kids, but a closed-off locale with people who only associated with town natives wouldn't do either.

Our new place is in a neighborhood near downtown, a short walk from my new school. My room is too bright, but maybe that means the future will be too. It has to be.

Velma promised it would. Not in those exact words, but she laid out a flawless argument for Coolsville in the multipage spreadsheet she sent when I told her Dad and I had decided to move. She made her hometown sound appealing. There are many reasons why Coolsville was the perfect choice: California is a great place for an up-and-coming band. We'd know people, and Coolsville High is huge, so Luna, Dusk, and I wouldn't feel "new" for too long. Best of all, it's excruciatingly boring.

"No ghosts," Velma swore on our final video call as I rolled up my band posters—the Cure, Siouxsie and the Banshees, Bauhaus, and more of my goth heroes—and secured them with rubber bands. "Just four built-in friends and a beach within a half-hour drive."

"That sounds nice," I admitted.

"You deserve nice," she said.

I didn't know how to respond to that, not after how my lifelong neighbors turned on my dad and me after what happened with the Ravencrofts. Nice had become a foreign concept to me. The only kindness I saw anymore was on the buffering screen of these video calls. In the texts and emails of this pen pal friendship we'd developed since Velma and her friends left town, after saving Oakhaven and unintentionally damning me at the same time.

I didn't expect to develop any sort of friendship with the people who shook up my life and then hopped back into their van to find another mystery to solve. The follow request from Velma on my now-private social media page was a surprise. I accepted it mainly to see the types of things she shared. I wanted to know if upheaval was all Mystery Inc. did, or if they had any sort of life outside of shattering mine.

I was bitter.

Velma was apologetic. The first time she reached out was with a message asking how I was doing. Her second, a comment on an old band practice video, complimenting the song. Her third, a like on a very old selfie; her fourth and fifth consecutive messages swearing the third was not her stalking me. Her sixth, a video that Scooby—her friend Shaggy's dog—accidentally filmed of himself licking and poking her phone with his snout, with an attached caption claiming:

Velma: See?!

Thorn: Sure, I totally believe you.

I included a rolling-eyes GIF.

Knowing her as I do now, I have to wonder if the

"accidental" like was an intentional ploy to get me to respond. Velma isn't cruel, but she's calculating. She told me she thought for days about how to check in on the Hex Girls and me after the incident in Oakhaven. She wasn't sure I would respond, but she wanted us to know they'd never meant for us to suffer from the fallout.

Her kindness made the shunning at home even more unbearable. I couldn't hold on to my resentment while Velma and her friends did everything possible to make up for the results of what they had unveiled.

As Velma and I moved from likes to messages to video chats, she became one of my only lifelines outside of my band. As I got closer to her and further away from most of the people around me, I slowly accepted that I had to leave Oakhaven. Soon, it was undeniable. I couldn't stay somewhere where the sight of me only reminded people of pain and betrayal.

Here I can start over. *We* can start over.

I push the window open a little further to air out the dust and refresh Eldritch. The sky reflects the pink of my room, mixed with the orange and purples of early sunset. The streets are emptying out as my new neighbors retreat for the evening, and soon no one's out except for a couple of people on the far corner. I can't see their faces in the fading light, but I don't need to. Their monochrome outfits and bold, colorful hair would stand out anywhere.

"Dusk!" I yell from the window. "Luna!"

My bandmates swivel their heads, searching for me. I

call out to them once more before racing downstairs to meet them. There's a flyer advertising a landscaping service taped to the door when I open it. I pull it down as they walk in, then drop it on the table for Dad to look at when he heads to order that pizza he promised.

"Your place is so far from the one my parents rented," Dusk complains as I let them in. I smile at her typically pessimistic greeting. She's a glass-half-empty type of person. Luna is a glass-half-full. I'm a glass drained dry as of late. Dusk tightens the neon green scrunchie holding her short, bleached blond curls in the shape of a mushroom cloud atop her head, and then pulls at the neck of the sweatshirt she's wearing, even though she's sweating in the heat.

"We had to take a bus to get here," Luna says as we head up to my room. "But it wasn't too bad. My mom already got me a metro pass, so I can come over anytime."

"I'll have to ask my dad for one," Dusk says. "If we have the budget for it."

"Yeah, tell me about it," I say when we reach the landing. "We don't have the money to fix *this* either yet." I open my bedroom door, unleashing the horror upon them.

"*Thorn,*" Dusk whispers, like somebody just died. She walks carefully around the minefield of cardboard, as if brushing a box accidentally might make the room explode and infect her with floral femininity.

"I know."

I push some of the unopened boxes aside with my foot to clear a space for us to sit down. Dusk joins me on the floor, but Luna pokes at my mess. "We could help you unpack if you want," she offers. Luna is always trying to make the best of any situation, and I knew this would be no different. "I helped Dusk a bit before we headed over here."

"That would be great," I say, "but you don't have to."

"What are sisters for?" Dusk says, despite her obvious disgust at our surroundings. She drags a box in front of her folded legs.

Luna already has one opened, having located a box cutter. She passes it to Dusk so she doesn't have to risk her long, glittering green nails clawing at the packing tape like I did. "Jackpot," she says as she reaches inside and pulls out my SO GOTH I WAS BORN BLACK tee.

I take it from her and then pull off my road-trip-reeking top to switch it out. "Can't lose track of this. Have you found yours yet?" I bury my nose in the collar of the shirt, breathing deep. It still smells like Oakhaven—pine woods and spice. It stirs something in me, and nostalgia threatens to bring me to the edge of something I never do: cry.

I'm just so glad Dusk and Luna are here. They didn't have to move with me. It would have spelled the end of the Hex Girls, our band, but they weren't the primary targets of the vitriol back home. They were only guilty by association. If they'd stayed, their lives could have gone back to normal without me. Instead, they chose to give up everything they knew so we could stick together.

"I found mine," Dusk says, "but Luna has unpacked everything and still hasn't found hers." She brings the same nails she wouldn't risk on the tape to her mouth and chews her way to a hangnail on her thumb. I know she wants to say more, but doesn't want to stress me out any further.

"It'll turn up," Luna says from the closet, where she's hanging the rest of the clothes from the box. The setting sun is now nearly the same deep red as her Afro.

Dusk hands me the box cutter before unpacking the box in front of her. "Oh," she says, sounding embarrassed. I lean forward to see what caused her reaction. Jars of herbs and a well-loved notebook rest inside. "It's your Wicca stuff." She rests her hands on the edge, seeming unsure what to do.

"Uh . . . we can just put that against the wall for now," I say. "I don't need it."

She nods and walks away from me. I cut open another three boxes to busy my hands. Neither of my friends say anything when they return to help me, and the silence is almost worse. There's nothing scandalous or incriminating in this trio of boxes, but my clothes feel like iron weights in my hands. My relief at my friends' presence is replaced with a reminder of why we're here.

"I saw the dog at the park earlier," Luna offers, breaking the awkward silence and thankfully changing the subject.

"Scooby?" I ask.

"Yeah, he was licking a fallen ice cream cone by the swing sets," she says. "I didn't see any of the others, though."

"I'm sure Shaggy was nearby if Scooby was there," I say. "He was probably getting more ice cream." My friends haven't spent as much time with Velma's friends—Shaggy,

Daphne, and Fred—as I have in their cameos on my video calls, but the food obsession of Shaggy and his loyal Great Dane became town legend when they tested the limits of "all you can eat" at the local diner.

"Probably." Luna smiles.

"Well, I saw a black cat near my new apartment," Dusk says. "I've been seeing them everywhere since we got here. I feel like this pink nightmare is another bad omen."

"A black cat isn't a bad omen," I say, opening another box. "It's goth solidarity."

"Yeah, well," Dusk starts, "this"—she gestures at the walls of my room—"isn't. First Luna loses her shirt, now you're living in a candy-coated fairy tale. What's next?"

"The pink isn't *that* awful," I hedge. I do have to live with it for the foreseeable future, after all. "It's gross, but it's not deadly."

"It's not so bad," Luna agrees. I mouth *thank you* at her when Dusk sighs and turns to look into the next box.

Despite Luna's backup, Dusk doubles down. "I have a bad feeling about this place," she says. "I know you have friends here, but I still think we should have chosen Seattle. Grunge is so much more our scene."

"We all have friends here," I say. "We have each other. And I know you'll like the Mystery Inc. crew once you get to know them better. They've been really nice to me. It won't be like it was when they came to Oakhaven. And Velma said they haven't told anyone here about what happened back home. Everything will be better now, I promise it will."

"Thorn," Luna says, and I can tell from her tone of voice that this isn't another peacemaking reassurance. She glances at Dusk, her downturned full lips showing me she's in agreement with our champion naysayer. "You can't run from your past forever."

I slice open another box in lieu of answering.

I can certainly try.

CHAPTER THREE

As I walk into Coolsville High School the next morning, I shove my hands in the pockets of my thinnest hoodie, the lightest item of clothing I own that's school dress code appropriate. It's so warm here. Still, the difference in weather between New England and California is small compared to the differences between my old single-building schoolhouse in Oakhaven and Coolsville High.

I weave my way between the hundreds of students in the open courtyard, repeating the directions the secretary in the administration building gave me to my newly assigned homeroom. This school is so big that the map on the back of my printed schedule fills the entire page. Several buildings are big enough to each contain my former schoolhouse twice over. It looks more like a college than a high school.

Classes don't start for another ten minutes, so no one follows me when I slip inside the building circled on my map. I find my homeroom at the end of the hall on the second floor.

"Ms. Bergman?" I address the woman behind the desk from the doorway. "I'm new. I was told to come see you before class?"

"Hi there." She beams, pushing her large rounded glasses up her freckled nose. "I remember a memo about you. What's your last name, sweetheart?"

"McKnight," I tell her, stepping fully into the room while she pokes at her keyboard. She must be an art teacher outside of morning homeroom assignment. Her classroom is covered in colors so bright and headache-inducing that they rival my new bedroom walls, but they don't feel nearly so suffocating here. I run my fingers along a rainbow of paint jars.

"Thorn?" Ms. Bergman asks. The shock on my face when I look at her must be confusing, because she adds, "That is your name, correct?"

"Yes," I confirm. "I just didn't expect you to call me that. It's not my given name."

"Oh," she says. "Well, it says you listed Thorn as your

preferred name on your intake forms. That's typically what your teachers will default to when referring to you. I can change it back?"

The bell rings and my new classmates filter into the room. "No," I say. "Thorn is perfect."

"No problem," she says. "If you stay up here while the others get settled, I'll introduce you and we'll get started with the day."

I don't answer, because I know she isn't actually giving me a choice. My preference would be to avoid any introduction at all. I've never been the New Kid before. I'd known all my former classmates since preschool. The only way I ever stood out in Oakhaven was self-inflicted by my clothes and music. Well . . . until the Ravencrofts. That's when I learned that being the center of attention is different when it's not by choice. I've muscled through stage fright at every gig the band has played, but this is a different kind of exposure.

"Good morning, everyone," Ms. Bergman starts. "We are in week three of the school year. You should all be well settled by now, so I'd like you to extend some kindness to our new student so that she feels equally at home here at Coolsville High. Thorn, would you like to introduce yourself?"

No, I wouldn't.

"Um," I say to no one in particular, my eyes studying the popcorn ceiling instead. "My name is Thorn McKnight. I moved here from a small town in Massachusetts—like super tiny, really boring." *Don't look it up,* I plead telepathically. "I play in a band called the Hex Girls with my best friends, Luna and Dusk. They . . . uh, they also moved here with me. That's pretty much it."

I look at Ms. Bergman, begging to be done with this. She smiles back at me, oblivious to my torture. "A band," she repeats. "So cool! Massachusetts must be very different from California. Is anyone willing to help Thorn navigate the school?"

"That's not necessary," I try. "I'm sure I can—"

"It's a big school," Ms. Bergman insists. "A friend is always a help, especially in your first few days."

"No," I insist. "It's really okay. I'll be fine."

"Nonsense," she says. "Look, we already have a volunteer."

I drag my eyes from the teacher's well-meaning face to the sole hand raised high above the sea of heads before me. The fingers are painted nearly the same pastel pink as my room. "I don't need anyone," I begin as my eyes travel downward, only to change my mind when I recognize the owner of the hand.

I'd know that perfectly styled red hair anywhere.

Daphne Blake, one of Velma's three closest friends, smiles as she watches the terror drain from my face. She lifts her backpack from the seat next to her, which she reserved for me. I gratefully plop into the chair, waiting for my racing heartbeat to return to normal. Ms. Bergman returns her focus to the class as a whole, finally leaving me alone.

"We looked for you before the bell," Daphne says as she plucks my schedule from my hands. "You haven't been responding to texts for the past few days. It's been stressing Velma out. She was worried you changed your mind and went back East."

"After we already spent all the money to get here?" I say. "No way. Our parents would kill us after how much we begged to move in the first place."

"I know," Daphne says, her lip-glossed smile widening. "We told her as much, but she said she couldn't think of another reason you wouldn't reply. Fred told her you were probably busy unpacking."

"I was," I confirm as Daphne reaches into her bag to grab some highlighters and then begins marking up my schedule. "But I had to get a new phone, too. Our old network doesn't have very good coverage here, so we switched." And I definitely could have—*should have*—texted the gang my new number like I did with the Hex Girls, but something kept me from hitting Send. Maybe because I can't shake the feeling that the promise of Coolsville is too good to be true.

"I'm sorry I didn't tell you all sooner," I say, genuinely meaning it. "I guess I just forgot in the chaos of the move." This part is less true, but I refuse to admit how many times I drafted a message to Velma only to delete it. I refuse to let anything endanger my future here, especially my growing feelings for someone who probably only sees me as a friend.

At first, I didn't feel anything other than friendship toward Velma. When Mystery Inc. was in Oakhaven, she was just the smartest member of the nosy group of kids disrupting my life. But as we talked more and more after her initial check-in, I learned that she was not just smart; she was brilliant. Not just nice; she was truly kind. And she was passionate about helping others, about standing by her friends, and about doing what was right, even if it was hard. Our scheduled phone call soon became the thing getting me through a long day, and I always made sure we had planned the next one before hanging up. It wasn't until I missed half a band practice this summer because I didn't want to get off a call that I had to face the fact that I had started to fall for her. She hasn't given me any indication that the feeling is mutual—or even if she's interested in girls—so I'm just going to have to keep it to myself . . . and Luna and Dusk, who know all my secrets.

"It's no big deal," Daphne says, pulling me from my thoughts. She grabs her phone and unlocks it, one hand still vandalizing my schedule, then hands it to me with a new contact input screen already open. I tap in my details as she puts the caps on her markers. "Blue is Freddie, green is Shaggy, orange is Velma, and purple is me," she says, handing my now-color-coded schedule back to me.

"Looks like we only share homeroom together, but that's every day and is basically for catching up on homework, so we'll have plenty of time to hang out." Daphne pauses, glancing at her lap to confirm what she's typing on her phone, then sliding it back in her pocket before Ms. Bergman catches her. "The others will help you and the girls settle in."

My own phone vibrates in my hoodie pocket. I poke it out enough to see the notification:

New Group Chat with (Maybe) Daphne and 3 others

> **Daphne (maybe):** I FOUND HER! Thorn got a new phone. Mystery solved.

"Thank you," I tell her as my phone vibrates a few more times.

"No problem," she says. "Now, on to more serious topics: When are we going to go buy you a warm-weather wardrobe? The black alone is going to be a battle against all this sun, but I love a challenge."

CHAPTER FOUR

There are no familiar faces in my next class, but for third period I have algebra with Fred, according to Daphne's color-coding. I cling to that as I maneuver my way across campus for the third time this morning. Students swerve around me, all so much faster than I am on the concrete pathways they've memorized and can navigate without a second thought. Most of them don't even watch where they're going.

This backfires on one boy. As I cut through a courtyard

to get to class, I see him bump into a statue of two Wild West–looking pioneers. His backpack splits open on the sharp base, sending books and papers scattering in front of the statue. Most of the other students just step around the new obstacles. I hurry forward.

"Are you okay?" I ask. I bend down to help gather the fluttering papers. The bell rings as I lower myself to the ground, but I ignore it.

"I'm fine," the boy says. "Don't," he adds sharply as he grabs a printout before I can catch it. "Leave it alone." He tries to shove his books back into the ripped bag.

"I was just trying to help," I say.

"I don't need it," he says. "Don't touch my things."

"Did you hit your head?" I bite out, annoyed now that I've made myself late for someone so ungrateful. The base certainly looks sharp enough to have caused a concussion. Or at least, it did. The part where the boy landed has crumbled a bit. Small pieces of old brick are littered among his fallen school supplies. "You broke it."

"It's an ancient piece of junk anyway," he says. He stuffs the last book back into his bag and stands up. As he rises, the split bag rips even further and spills everything back out. He swears and kicks the statue before turning his anger back on me. "What are you still here for?"

"I—" I start, faltering. I don't know anymore. The instinct to be a Good Samaritan has certainly left me. I should go now. I'm already late. But I'm mad too. I don't deserve to be treated like this just because the boy is frustrated.

"You what?" he demands, a cruel grin spreading on his face. "Dead cat got your tongue, goth girl?"

"Watch it," I warn him.

He steps back as I step forward, but doesn't shut up, even when he bumps up against the statue again. He turns his head, seeming to glare at the bronze pairing, but his words are still aimed at me. "I told you I didn't need your help."

"Yeah," I agree. "But you certainly need someone's help."

He opens his mouth to insult me again, but both of us are distracted by something coming from the fallen bricks. A small metallic-looking cloud rises from the dents the rubble made in the grass. It's weird-looking, not quite matching the statue it came from.

Unnatural. *Super*natural.

I know it's going to happen before it does, so I ignore the boy's protests as I pull him away just before the statue topples. We stumble back as it hits the ground. The weird discoloration dissipates immediately, leaving no evidence behind except a smear of gold dust on the boy's now-flattened backpack.

I leave him alone with the wreckage. I have to. The more I look at it, the more I wonder . . . what if it was my fault? Did I topple that statue because I couldn't control my anger? This is why I left magic in Oakhaven. It's too dangerous. I have to let it go before it destroys my life again.

When I finally reach math class, the teacher seems distracted by the pile of homework in front of him. He gestures toward the desks without looking up, sparing me another classroom introduction. I search for Fred, knowing from the group chat that he's saved a seat for me.

What I'm not expecting is to see Luna sitting next to him. They're deep in conversation when I join them, having already reconnected in their homeroom. "There's a talent show audition this afternoon!" Luna tells me as I slide into the desk behind her. "Fred says talent scouts from Los Angeles have come to the final show the past few years. We have to audition! It's just a matter of deciding which song." Out of habit, she pulls a strand of her 'fro down to rub between her thumb and forefinger while she deliberates. "I should text Dusk about song choices."

I nod absentmindedly, my heart still racing from the situation with the statue.

Fred twists in his chair to greet me. He looks like he dressed for a day at the beach instead of an air-conditioned classroom, but then again, so do most of my new classmates. Even Luna is a wearing a deep maroon crop top, already at home. I long ago tied my hoodie around my waist. Eager for a distraction, I point at the small strip of fabric tied around Fred's neck. "Does that help with the heat?" I ask. "Does the breeze catch it and help cool you down or something?"

Fred tilts his blond head down, like that will give him a better vantage point to view his own neck. "Oh, my ascot?" he asks. "Did Daph tell you to comment on it?" I quickly say no, but he's already texting her a series of siren emojis, calling her the fashion police. She replies immediately:

Daphne: Is this about the ascot? Again?

"I know it's outdated," Fred says as he continues his unserious text war with Daphne. "But it's an ode to town history. The founders of Coolsville wore ascots, an elevated version of the bandannas miners wore around their necks to battle dust and sweat while they worked."

"I didn't mean to cause a rift between you and Daphne," I joke. "I don't want to harm your relationship."

"There's no me and Daphne," Fred says quickly, tugging on his ascot as if it's overheating him now instead of keeping him cool, his cheeks bright red. "Daph and I are just friends."

"I meant in general," I clarify. I know Velma was the one who suggested we move here, but I don't want our presence to upset any preexisting dynamics.

"We should do our namesake song," Luna interjects, clearly not paying attention to my discussion with Fred. "It's a good introduction to our band for a new audience and we can play it from memory."

I nod. "That sounds great."

"What *sounds great*," comes the teacher's voice from the front of the classroom, "is paying attention to these slides so you don't fail this class and force me to deal with you all for another semester." He glares at us as Fred and Luna turn around. The other students chuckle lightly. Math has never really been my best subject, so I devote myself to it for the rest of the period.

Luna doesn't share another class with me today, but we'll both be in band with Dusk on alternating days, so I wish her luck as I head off. I don't know anyone in fourth or fifth period. At least being with people I knew, there was some distraction from the curious glances in my direction. Alone, it's impossible not to feel like everyone's staring at me.

It's weird feeling so lonely surrounded by so many people. It's hard not to feel like they know something is wrong with me.

By the time sixth period rolls around, I'm grateful to see Shaggy's unkempt mop of hair and wide grin as I give my second-to-last introduction of the day, even though assigned seating means that I have to sit on the opposite side of the room from him.

Just as I take my seat near the window, a loud thump startles me—and the rest of the class. Two muddy paws slide against the polished glass. "Scooby?" I know he can't hear me, but he still looks toward me and begins barking in delight.

"Mr. Rogers!" scolds the teacher. "How many times have you been told not to let that dog wander around the campus?"

"Am I supposed to leave him in the van?" Shaggy asks. "That's inhumane!"

"Your dog is not human."

"Neither are the characters in this book you assigned to us, but you seem to find their lives pretty important."

The teacher sighs. "Do not compare your dog to *Animal Farm*, Mr. Rogers."

Shaggy continues to go back and forth with the teacher until the entire class is laughing. It takes all the attention off Scooby, and by association, me. I sigh and sit back. There is so much going on at Coolsville High, there is no way anyone will care about the new kids for long.

CHAPTER FIVE

One more class. One more introduction.

As I begin my seventh iteration of the same speech, it feels like a song I've rehearsed so much I could play it in my sleep. I don't even need to focus to know what I'm going to say. I let my eyes wander across the room as I repeat my speech, and almost trip over my words and say my name is Velma when I spot her.

I only half hear the thank-you and dismissal to find a seat when I finish. I'm so embarrassed as I maneuver through the maze of rectangular desks covered with beakers and test tubes to reach Velma at the back of the room. I knew from my Daphne-annotated schedule that I'd share this class with her. The sight of her shouldn't scramble my words so much.

She drags her bag off the stool next to her as I approach. "Hi," she says, sounding much less flustered than I do. Her expression is positive but subdued. "I traded seats with someone so that we could be lab partners," she says. "I hope you don't mind."

"No," I say, biting back a smile so big I'm certain it could crack my black lipstick. "I mean, of course I don't mind. I'd love to be lab partners."

"Okay, good," Velma says. She looks away from me and brushes her short brown bob back with both hands and then realigns her glasses on her ears before returning her hands to the desk. "You said science wasn't one of your strongest subjects, so I figured being partners might help."

"Because you're so smart," I tease.

"I wouldn't say—" she starts, at the same time as I say, "I just meant that—"

"You go first," she says.

"I just meant that you have done so much to ease the stress of this move," I say. "You thought of every possibility. I appreciate it, I hope you know."

"Thank you," she says. "It was nothing, really."

"And I'm sorry I didn't reach out with my new number sooner," I add. I sit down and scoot toward the desk, attempting to make sense of the worksheet in front of me.

I glance up at her. "Daphne told me you were worried."

"I wasn't worried," Velma says. It comes out sharply, feeling like the unexpected slam of a door. She doesn't look at me as she speaks, her head tilting forward so her hair covers her reddening cheeks a bit better. "It was just out of character for you. You text a lot, so I wondered what had changed. I wasn't worried," she repeats. "Sometimes my friends exaggerate." Her pencil taps the desk in rhythm with her words.

"Yeah, sure," I acquiesce, confused. "I just wanted to apologize."

"No need," she says. "Did you want some help with the worksheet? I can explain where we are in this lesson if you want."

I let out a relieved breath. "I'd love that. Thanks."

This is the first time I've interacted with Velma in person since she came to Oakhaven last year. I was worried that the ease we'd developed around each other virtually might not translate to real life, but after the initial awkwardness, the hour we spend studying together is easily the most comfortable I've felt all day.

"The auditorium is over there, on the other side of the cafeteria. It's kind of out of sight if you aren't looking for it," Velma says as we walk across the now-empty courtyard after class. "It isn't obvious . . ." she adds, trailing off.

"I would have assumed it was the biggest building, because of the space it needs for the theater seats," I say. "Except—"

"Except all the buildings on campus are pretty big," Velma finishes.

"Exactly," I say, laughing even though the campus is more intimidating than amusing. I swivel my head to see if the broken statue is visible from where we are. Mercifully, I don't spot it. I don't know if Velma's schedule brought her anywhere near it before science class, but if it did, she doesn't seem to have found it suspicious enough to comment on. I don't think we could have avoided the topic if we had had to pass it on our way over here.

I only need to avoid the statue until the newness of it is gone. Until *my* newness is gone. Too much is riding on this move for me to screw things up this early.

"I know the others are probably already waiting for us inside, but I wanted to take a minute to show you this." Velma walks ahead of me and disappears around the corner of a building. I hurry to catch up. When I do, what I see makes me stop in my tracks. It's not the statue or the theater. I can see the auditorium clearly now, but it pales in comparison to the sight right before me.

Blossoming flowers and ripening fruits and vegetables climb upward and outward from a large plot directly across from the theater entrance. It's not as big as the school's football field, but it's easily a quarter or a third as long, bigger than any backyard I've seen in Coolsville so far. There's even a greenhouse with a beautiful trellis wrapped around it, both nearly gothic in their architecture and covered with grapevines.

"A garden," I whisper, as if it's a mirage I might scare away by acknowledging its presence.

"A community garden," Velma clarifies. "It's run by students. You can sign up for a volunteer shift."

"Right now?" I ask, eager to bury my hands in the earth, a hobby I wasn't sure the move would allow me to resume, since our new house doesn't have a very big yard. Dusk, Luna, and I are eco-goths. We embrace the dark clothes and general goth aesthetic but also consider nature in everything we do. We only buy our clothes secondhand or from small brands that are transparent about their practices. The same with our makeup and accessories. Dusk especially has gotten great at minor mending and alterations to our clothes, so we reuse old outfits rather than throw them out. Recycling and renewable resources are important to us. I've loved gardening since I was twelve, and used a lot of herbs in my Wicca practice, before . . .

Velma laughs. Her eyes close as she tilts her small face toward the sun. When she looks at me, she brushes at her hair and fixes her glasses like earlier. "We have another commitment right now," she reminds me.

"Right," I say. I quickly walk past the tempting greenery to the theater door. I pull it open and hold it as Velma hurries to catch up on her shorter legs. "But maybe after?"

"The after-school shift should have some gardeners out

there when we're done, yeah," she confirms.

"Awesome."

"Thorn!" Luna calls from a line that's formed along the far wall leading to the stage. The rest of Velma's friends sit in the aisle seats near the line.

As we get closer, I hear Shaggy bribing Scooby into silence with a sleeve of crackers. "They can't know you're in here, buddy," he reminds him. Scooby opens his mouth in excitement at the sight of Velma and me. Shaggy shakes the whole sleeve out on the floor to distract him.

"Where's Dusk?" I ask as I join Luna against the wall and Velma sits in the open seat next to Daphne.

"Not here yet," Luna says, "but she shouldn't be far behind you. I already signed us up. We're act number thirteen. I told them what instruments we'll need. They said they have the right ones. I just hope they're tuned correctly." Luna has a habit of rambling on gig days. It's the only time I ever see her unable to maintain her normal go-with-the-flow energy.

I nod, rolling my shoulders to shake out the preperformance nerves. "Have you met everybody yet?" I ask, gesturing to Velma and her friends.

"Thorn," Luna says, and laughs lightly. "We did go through the exact same experience in Oakhaven, in case you forgot. I may not have texted Velma all summer like you did, but I do remember the whole gang."

"Plus we have home ec together," Daphne adds.

"Did she color-code your class schedule too?" I ask Luna.

"Color-coding?" Velma turns on her friend. "I thought

40

that was my thing. Stealing my moves now, are we?"

"Don't worry, Velms," Daphne says. "I won't steal *everything.*"

"What's that supposed to mean?" Velma asks, hands reaching back to smooth her already-sorted hair again. Daphne just sticks her tongue out at her.

"Dusk says she had to stop by the admin office, but she's on her way now," Fred says, without looking up from his phone.

"They added you guys to the group chat?" I ask. I realize haven't looked at my phone since spotting Velma in chemistry. Luna nods.

"Sorry we didn't have more time to hang out before you guys started today," Daphne pauses her teasing to say. "We're not allowed to go on any more unchaperoned road trips out of state until we're eighteen. Otherwise we would have come visit sometime in the past year."

"We only almost died twice," Fred complains. "Statistically, we survived more often than not. That should count for something!"

Velma giggles. "That's not an accurate way to cite statistics, Fred."

Fred lets out an exasperated groan, dropping his head on Daphne's shoulder. "Well, this travel ban sucks. Nothing ever happens in Coolsville."

"This place *sucks,*" Dusk unknowingly agrees from a distance. She's storming so determinedly toward us in her spiked boots that I fear for the exposed toes of some of

41

the sandal wearers in line. Fred gives her a thumbs-up in solidarity. "I am the only one who doesn't share a class with any of you," she says. "I went to the office, but they refused to change my schedule."

"We have band," Luna offers.

"And lunch," I try.

"Everyone shares lunch," she says, but her voice isn't as vitriolic. It's defeated. "I'm alone for six out of seven classes."

I lock eyes with Luna above Dusk's morose head, but I can't think of anything to fix this. I'm sure Dusk is viewing this as yet another bad omen regarding our move here. If we botch our audition, that will only add fuel to the fire.

Dusk cheers up some when she spots Scooby lying on the floor in front of our friends, the four of them lightly resting their feet on his back as if he's a furry ottoman. She squats down to let him lick her hand.

She only stands up again when the first act is called to play. It's another girl band, playing a slightly stripped-down version of a pop song that was big this summer. "They're good," Dusk says. "Jordan said she had a band, but I didn't know they were auditioning too."

"Jordan?" I ask.

"The lead vocalist," Dusk says, pointing to a white girl with an ombré pixie cut, the brown of her hair fading to platinum blond at the tips. "We have physics together." Jordan and her bandmates finish to strong applause, and they bow to the crowd before exiting the stage.

A slightly raunchy puppet show takes the stage next,

earning a lot of laughs but really pushing the limits of what is audience appropriate for a high school talent show. Daphne admires the craftsmanship of the puppets, complimenting the presumably handmade outfits, starting another lighthearted fashion debate between her and Fred.

"Is arguing how they flirt?" I whisper to Velma. She snort-laughs so loud it causes the tap dancer onstage to miss a step. I keep my comments to myself after that, but let the joy of making her laugh warm me as we wait for our turn.

"Act thirteen: The Hex Girls," a voice announces over the loudspeaker after about thirty minutes of auditions.

Our friends cheer us as we head to the stage. "We can do this," Luna says. We approach the borrowed instruments. Dusk's frustration fades away as she settles at the drums. The happy sigh she lets out as she tests the drumsticks is a far cry from the disgruntled noises she made at the back of the line. Music always makes her feel better. I would be so much more comfortable with my own guitar, but I try to repress the rising doubts creeping toward the forefront of my mind. I can't allow anything but the music in.

"On three," I confirm with the girls. They both nod from their stations, Dusk at the drum set and Luna at the keys. I sling the guitar around my neck and step forward to the microphone.

One . . . two . . . three.

I sing the opening line into the microphone. "The Hex Girls," our titular song, is a love spell cast with instruments. It's sultry and seductive and so much fun to perform, especially for an audience of people our own age instead of tourist families in pioneer garb.

Dusk and Luna repeat the hook, which promises enchantment through our upcoming verses, while I strum the guitar. I rejoin them for the second part of the chorus. I let the music take me away, becoming lightheaded and enraptured by the sounds around me. The lyrics of our song are about putting a spell on the audience, but when I'm onstage I always feel like a spell falls over me instead. Music and singing help me forget the world—the disaster in Oakhaven, being the new kid, fighting with my dad—and find inner peace.

As we start the chorus again, I can see some of the crowd of waiting acts and curious classmates start mouthing the words along with us. It's such a rush I can't help but look at my best friends as we sing, to make sure they're seeing it too.

They definitely are. Dusk's rage has bled out into her drumbeat, and now that she's witnessed the response to her performance, she's glowing with pride. I have to remind myself to look back at the crowd as we start the bridge. I serenade the audience as Luna's fingers play a haunting melody on the keyboard.

When we start the chorus for the final time, even more of the crowd is quietly jamming along, making the last line even more powerful. Luna, Dusk, and I finish in unison. The cheers from the crowd sound louder than they did for a lot of the other acts. The Mystery Inc. crew even leap to their feet, clapping and yelling for an unnecessary encore.

I'm smiling so wide it hurts as we exit the stage hugging each other happily. It feels good to return to my roots like this, a sentiment that is almost too on the nose when we push out the auditorium doors as the next act begins and I see the community garden.

"Give me a moment," I tell the girls, breaking away from them to approach the students gardening. "Hi," I say. "Could you tell me how to sign up for a volunteer shift here?"

A girl wearing a straw hat labeled PROPERTY OF COOLSVILLE HIGH blinks up at me. "Here?" she repeats, looking me up and down. "Are you sure?" Her tone is doubtful, like she thinks I'm playing some sort of prank.

"Mary Allyn!" the other gardener snaps. "Sorry. She can be a little judgmental."

I laugh it off, still riding my performance high. "I get it, because of the all-black," I say. "My friends and I are actually eco-goths. We like the dark aesthetic, but everything we do is about sustainability. Our clothes are as ethically sourced as possible, we recycle, and I love nature. I'm even a vegan."

"Oh!" the first gardener, Mary Allyn, says, clearly surprised yet again. She shakes her hands free of dirt and grabs a tablet enclosed in a waterproof case. "In that case, you can sign up on this. Volunteer hours count toward your community service requirement for graduation, too!" After double-checking that I have my newly assigned student number correct, I add it in and sign up for a shift tomorrow afternoon.

I wave goodbye and rejoin the girls. "The gang had to get

going, but they said they'll see you tomorrow," Luna says.

"You'll all see each other tomorrow," Dusk grumbles. "Except me."

I guess the performance high has worn off for her. "You guys wanna come over?" I ask. The house is still too much of a disaster to do anything fun, but the three of us have never struggled to find ways to entertain each other.

"I still have unpacking to do," Dusk says.

"Since we missed the school bus to audition, I'd better get going too," Luna adds.

"Yeah, that's fine," I say, not fully meaning it. "But we're still down for band practice tomorrow, right?"

They both agree and then head for the bus stop while I start in the opposite direction, trying not to feel like this split-up is anything more than practical. It's impossible to spend every waking moment together. I guess I just thought they'd like to celebrate a successful audition together.

I look up as I crest another hill and see a billboard with a Coolsville tourism ad: RELAX THE DAY AWAY, it encourages against a beach background. EVERYTHING'S CHILL IN COOLSVILLE! I try to take it to heart. If walking home alone sometimes is the worst thing I'll face in Coolsville, then this move has accomplished exactly what I needed it to.

When I approach my new house, the door opens before I reach for it.

"I thought you were working today," I say, surprised to see my dad standing in the doorway.

"I left early so I could be here when you got home," Dad

says. "You're late. Did you get lost?"

"No," I say, shucking my shoes off. "There were auditions for the talent show. I didn't know you'd be here or I would have texted."

"Don't worry about it," he says. "That's great! Did you make the cut?"

"I won't know for a few days."

He just looks at me for a moment, not doubting the honesty of my answers but not asking me anything else either. I wish I could look at him with the same level of trust. I know he wants to ask me more about my first day. I almost want to let him. I used to tell him about my days without him having to ask. But even though today went well, I still can't forget why I had to be the new kid in the first place. If it weren't for his scheme in Oakhaven, we would probably still be there.

So instead of saying more, I retreat to the pink room.

CHAPTER SIX

Getting your hands dirty is the antidote to everything.

I open the dirt-covered palm of my gloved hand and extend it to Mary Allyn for more seeds. She's been much nicer today. The boy who was with her yesterday afternoon is not scheduled for today's shift, but another girl has joined us in his stead, so we are making great progress in prepping the plant beds for the upcoming harvest.

"The grapes should be ready to pick next week," says the new girl, who introduced herself as Kailey. To me, they look good enough to eat already, glistening on the vines. Behind the sharp points of the wrought iron trellis, the greenhouse holds the more sensitive crops. This garden is truly a triumph, especially only a few weeks into the new school year.

I want to ask so many questions about it, like who tended it over the summer when everyone was gone and if that's a position I could sign up for next year. I want to ask both girls more about themselves—how they like Coolsville, what kind of music they're into, what kind of movies they watch. Maybe finding some common ground will make me feel a little less like an alien.

I should feel more confident about my place here, especially after seeing the callback list this morning.

Jordan, Dusk's physics classmate, turned out to be just as commanding offstage as she was behind a microphone. She flitted among the other students waiting for the callback sheet with such ease it seemed to make her pixie cut nearly fairylike, as if she cut it for speed over style. The odds on the acts that would make the list changed as she passed. Optimistic conversations became shaky and nervous after she interjected her opinion.

None of the other hopefuls really spoke to us as we waited. I sat on a concrete half wall, hiding my crossed fingers in the folds of my pleated red skirt.

"Do you think they'll take two bands this year?" one kid asked.

"There's enough time in the program," another said.

50

"They took three the year before last," a third added.

"Yes," Jordan said, her eyes shooting over to me. "But talent scouts attend the show every year, so they should only take the best of the best."

I tried to hold my tongue. I waited, swallowing down the words twice before giving in. The topic had almost changed when I finally spit them out. "What's that supposed to mean?" I asked Jordan.

"What's *what* supposed to mean?" she asked. Her eyes were ice blue and just as cold, despite the faux innocence in her voice.

"Thorn," Luna said, pulling at my elbow with her mesh-gloved hand. "Let's not."

I glared at Jordan. I resisted the urge to hop down from my spot to tug at the thread further, especially when I saw Dusk cracking each of her knuckles with a manicured thumb. Dusk has always been the easiest to anger out of our group, and I could tell she was practically dissociating in her attempt to not get involved. She stared glassy-eyed past us all, laser focused on the empty slot on the noticeboard where the list of callbacks would eventually be placed.

"I think it's cool that you guys auditioned on your first day here," Jordan said in an overly empathetic tone, like she was complimenting a toddler's scribbles. "Takes a lot of confidence. I applaud you. What's your band name again?"

"The Hex Girls," Luna said.

Jordan chuckled lightly, rolling her eyes as she looked around the other hopefuls again. "Of course," she said. "The song was kind of obvious about that. Repeated it in the chorus about a dozen times."

I tightened my knuckles on the edge of the wall, resisting the urge to explain to her how a chorus works in my most condescending tone. Still, my gaze crept back to Luna, asking permission to reconsider her plea for pacifism. But I didn't have to.

"It's up!" Dusk yelled. The crowd perked up at her announcement. The glass lid of the noticeboard was being locked back in place by a teacher who then quickly fled the onslaught of several dozen teenagers closing in.

I locked arms with the girls and shouldered through. Disappointed swearing and a few muffled sobs blended with excited shouts, all spinning into a symphony of anxiety as we stepped closer. *Please, please, please.*

"Thorn?" Mary Allyn asks in a tone that implies she's repeated my name a few times.

"Sorry," I apologize, shaking away the memory and passing her the trowel she was reaching for. "I was thinking about callbacks."

"For the talent show thingy, right?" she asks, pointing the shovel toward the theater. The action accidentally flicks some wet soil on my face. I carefully wipe it off my cheek without messing up my eyeliner.

"Yeah, my band made the list," I say. "We go for round two tomorrow and then we'll find out if we made the show line-up."

"That's cool," she says. She tightens her strawberry-blond

hair in her high ponytail, seemingly unbothered about the dirt she leaves on the ends. "You know," she begins, like she's only somewhat sure about sharing a secret with me, "I have to admit that you've surprised me."

I nod in lieu of acknowledging the obvious. I'm used to this. As a goth—and as a Black goth in particular—I'm used to people making assumptions about me solely based on how I look. It feels good to command attention on my own terms, for something I'm proud of. This isn't like magic; there's nothing to be ashamed about in my appearance. My wardrobe and makeup have never hurt anybody.

"You didn't seem like the type of person who would want to help out at the garden, is all," Mary Allyn continues, apparently unable to help herself.

"I guess I like the opportunity to subvert expectations."

"Is that why you hang out with *them*?" Kailey asks as she returns from the greenhouse with empty pots to repot the plants that won't survive even the mild California winter without being moved indoors.

"Kailey," Mary Allyn warns, "we said we weren't gonna mention that."

I wait for them to continue, but neither of them speaks for a minute that stretches out to what feels like an hour to me. At superspeed, my mind spins a prize wheel of all the other things the two of them could have found curious or lacking about me. I toy with the pot in my hands to keep my mouth shut, attempting to read the brand label beneath the PROPERTY OF COOLSVILLE HIGH scribbled in thick permanent marker over it. It's Green-something, but that doesn't really narrow things down in the world of garden supplies.

"My band?" I finally ask. My fingernails grip so tight in my gloves I think I can feel phantom soil embed itself under my nails from the dirty palms that came before me. I breathe through a rush of indignation that didn't surface at the judgment of my personal aesthetic. They can say whatever they want about me, but if they're taking issue with my best friends—

"No," Mary Allyn says, maybe sensing my rising anger, "not them. Eco-goths, you said. They like plants too, right?"

"Yes," I say. My grip on the pot loosens.

"Cool with nature, cool with us," she confirms.

"Not your bandmates," Kailey echoes. She bites her lip and looks up at Mary Allyn, who shakes her head, before continuing. "The mystery makers," she says.

"Mystery Inc.?" I clarify.

They nod in unison, stopping as soon as they know I understand them. Like they're worried someone might overhear a verbal confirmation. They double down on the task at hand, quiet now that they've thrown me completely. I think back to Kailey's question and honestly don't understand why she asked it.

I thought the Mystery Inc. crew were quintessential Coolsville. They could model for one of the tourism billboards around town. A bunch of normal, modestly dressed white kids and a cute dog. Intelligent, kindhearted, supportive. They are everything this colorful town should be going for. So it's odd to hear them discussed in the same wary and apprehensive tones my new gardening pals used when I signed up the other day. Is there something wrong with the compost fumes here? Why are these two so suspicious?

I drop back on my heels. "You thought I wouldn't be helpful in the garden because you saw me with them," I say, dumbfounded. I still don't get it.

"Well," Kailey says, dragging out the word into multiple syllables.

"It's not really in their nature to be helpful," Mary Allyn says.

"More like meddlesome," Kailey finishes.

I begin to pack fresh soil back into the pot in front of me, not sure what else I can possibly say. I'm so confused. "I do like helping," I say, feeling a bit like a kid insisting they just love vegetables after they got caught stuffing green beans into their pocket. The idea of the most suspicious thing about me being my association with Mystery Inc. is so surreal I have no idea what to do with myself.

"We know that now," Mary Allyn says. "That's why I told Kailey maybe you just didn't know the truth about them."

"The truth?" I ask.

"That they're dangerous," Kailey says. My mind pulls up the image of the four of them using Scooby as a footrest at the theater yesterday. *Dangerous* is the last word I would associate with any of them. "Like Fred Jones," she continues.

"He uses connections to get them out of trouble for things that are entirely his fault. He's been banned from several stores in town for misusing products to make elaborate contraptions on private property, but he never gets in trouble for it. He always finds somewhere else to shop. I don't know how he does it."

"And Daphne Blake," Mary Allyn adds.

"Yeah," Kailey says. "Miss Moneybags. Maybe that's how they get off each time. You know, she has a soft spot for Fred."

"It's true," Mary Allyn continues. "They've all been best friends since before that dog was even born. Can't remember a time they weren't getting into trouble together. They're always looking for problems where there aren't any. They refuse to let anything go. Daphne misuses her anchor seat in broadcasting class to snoop. I heard she even stuck her nose where it didn't belong last summer at her journalism internship and got sent home early. Something happened at a private island and a small town down south. Even her family's money wasn't enough to get her out of that, I guess."

"Was it a southern town?" Kailey asks. "I thought it was more north."

"Does it really matter?" I ask in a tone of nearly manic disinterest. I already didn't like where the conversation was going, but this direction is even worse.

"You're right," Kailey says. "The details don't really matter as much as making sure you know to protect yourself from their trouble. Mary Allyn was worried you might get offended if we warned you. That's why she didn't want to say anything. But everyone knows about them, so it wouldn't be fair to not tell you, in my opinion."

She raises her eyebrows at me, seeking validation, I guess. "Yeah," I say, the word tasting as disgusting on my tongue as this soil would. "You're doing me a favor. Letting me know who to avoid in the future." *You two, for example.*

"Exactly!" Mary Allyn says, letting out a relieved breath. "I'm glad you understand. Norville Rogers isn't so bad. I can't even blame him for going by that nickname, honestly. The weirdest thing about him is how he drags that dog everywhere."

"Velma Dinkley is actually really nice," Kailey says. "There's not much to say about her other than her loyalty to the others. She's totally the smartest person in the entire school, not just in her grade. I guess that's the weirdest part of it for me. If she's so smart, she should know better than to risk her future by hanging around those types of people. Unless . . ."

"Unless?" I prompt.

"Unless there's something off about her, too."

CHAPTER SEVEN

The pink dungeon's size earns point in its favor with the loss of an actual garage to hold band practice in.

Thankfully, Dusk's drum kit is a nesting one designed for small spaces. She has several younger siblings, so space was an issue at her house even before they moved. She unpacks and assembles her kit in contented silence.

I think it would annoy me to constantly disassemble and reassemble my instrument every single time I wanted to use it, but Dusk has always liked puzzles. She's happiest when everything is in its proper place. She's less interested in how things work—unlike Luna—but the task of putting stuff together is one of the few things that can chill her hair-trigger temper.

Luna has a portable keyboard too, but it's not her only instrument. She lifts my bedroom window open a little higher to tempt more flying victims into Eldritch's traps. "Not too much," Dusk says without looking up from her drum set. "You'll let out all the cold air."

"Okay, *Dad*," Luna says, laughing.

"I'm on Dusk's side," I admit. "It's too hot for early fall." The thermostat is barely set that low, but adjusting to the heat is going to take time for my East Coast bones. "I didn't think it would still be this warm by the time we got here."

"That's because you weren't thinking about the weather at all," Luna says.

Dusk does a ba-dum-tss comedy beat on her finished drums and both my friends laugh at me. "Stop," I say, dragging out the word as Luna settles in the semicircle we've made on the floor of my mostly unpacked bedroom.

"Are we still pretending that a short, nerdy brunette had no influence on your sales pitch of Coolsville?" Luna asks.

"You're having fun here, don't lie," I remind her.

"I do love the opportunities available," she confesses. "It's nice to have actual choices for extracurriculars and an academic focus outside of just Advanced Placement. Coolsville High has more science and math class options than we had *teachers* in Oakhaven."

"That's great, Luna," I say. I pull my phone out of my pocket and unlock it. Still no new notifications. I try to covertly slip my phone back, but I'm caught.

"See?" Dusk nods at me. "You aren't even listening to us you're so distracted."

"This is not about Velma!"

"I never mentioned her by name," Luna points out. "We could have been talking about any short, nerdy brunette in the entire state of California."

"Strike two," Dusk says, nodding solemnly.

I pull my song notebook out of my backpack. "I'm here to work, not to gossip," I say. "If you're fine with failing our callback, that's on you, but I'm a professional." The girls get in a few more taunts, but we eventually start warming up on our respective instruments.

"Are we sticking with 'The Hex Girls' song for this?" Luna asks. She's pulled out her own notebook that she uses to brainstorm our five-, ten-, and twenty-year plans for global stardom. Luna is easygoing about most things, but there's nothing on earth she takes more seriously than our public performances. I'm glad she's locking in, though, if it saves me from further interrogation about Velma.

"I think we should," I say, "at least for the callback. For consistency."

"We should pick something else for the actual show," Dusk says. "Something new," she adds, her eyes going starry with the possibilities. She reaches for my song notebook, flipping it open before I can stop her.

"Give it back!" I say, lunging as she lifts the notebook higher above my grabby hands.

"Thorn!" Dusk says in a shocked and disappointed tone that I'd expect more from a parent or teacher than my best friend. "I'm just trying to see what you've written lately." She passes my notebook to Luna instead of back to me. "Since when have you started being cagey about unfinished lyrics?"

Since I stopped writing lyrics entirely.

Dusk is right. I have never been secretive about my songbook with them before. I write most of our songs, but I've always valued their input in the drafting process. This band is not a dictatorship. We listen to each other.

Listening. That's what Dusk and Luna offer me when they hand my notebook back. "I haven't been able to write anything new for months," I admit, even though I'm sure they realized that flipping through the pages. "Not since before we left Oakhaven."

"Is it related to . . ." Luna trails off. She's staring at the corner of my room where the half-open box containing all my Wicca stuff rests untouched from the day we arrived.

"I don't know," I say. I'm afraid to go anywhere near the box, physically or mentally. "It's probably just stress. We had so much to plan and keep track of preparing for this move and now we're here and—well, you know?"

"Yeah," Luna says, mercifully accepting my nonsense nonanswer. "I get you."

"We'll do 'The Hex Girls' for the callback and maybe you'll have something new by the show," Dusk agrees. "If not, we've got plenty of great songs to introduce to a new audience."

Luna nods. "Exactly."

"Thanks," I say. We get back to practicing. I attempt to jot something down in the quiet moments, but even with the welcome return of quality band time, nothing surfaces. I pull out my phone to check it once again, anything to distract myself. Still nothing.

I don't want to dwell on my writer's block. I'm terrified it's more than just a block. It feels bigger than that, like it's a wall, equal to the one I built around magic to keep it from following me across the country to this fresh start. I can't tear that wall down, even for my writing. I shouldn't be chipping at it. The consequences would be too severe. Most days I wake still tasting the smoke of Oakhaven's ruin on my tongue.

But how can I lead the Hex Girls if I'm too terrified to think about magic? The unknown used to be my inspiration; now it's my albatross. It's embarrassing to be a goth afraid of things that go bump in the night.

I pull out my phone again.

"Add another tally to your counter, Luna," Dusk says, but she's pointing right at me.

"Good catch," Luna says. She adds a line in the margin of her notebook, a crossing tally across four lines she had sketched earlier without me noticing. "Bingo! I win! Or whatever you say when you hit five in a tracker like this."

"What are you guys tracking?" I ask.

"It's your phone check counter," Dusk says. "It's not entirely accurate, though, because we only started counting halfway through practice."

"I've pulled it out five times?"

"Just since we've started counting," Dusk repeats.

I put my phone underneath me and make a show of sitting on it. "I'm sorry," I say. "I didn't realize I was checking it that often. I'm just waiting on an important message."

"From?" Luna prompts.

"A reporter," I confess. "I wasn't sure if I should mention it before it was set, but Daphne said *The Daily Babbler* was interested in doing a welcome feature on us. We could be in the local paper!"

"No way!" Dusk shrieks. She shoves me off my phone and moves it to the center of our semicircle, grinning at it like it's a winning lottery ticket. "Is it on silent? We need to make sure it makes a noise if you get an email. Or a text. How are they going to contact you?"

"Probably email," I say.

"This is so cool," Dusk says. She finds the silence button on my phone and turns it off before replacing the device face up on the floor in front of her.

"It is," Luna agrees, "but I'm a little bummed it wasn't who I thought it would be."

"You're disappointed we might be interviewed by a reporter?" I ask.

"No, of course not," Luna says. "That's great for us. I just thought it might be a solution for your writer's block instead.

You know what they say about an artist in love. There's no better inspiration."

Dusk cracks up, falling back on the floor and making kissy noises.

"Oh, shut up," I grumble, my cheeks reddening.

CHAPTER EIGHT

"Mr. Rogers," an annoyed voice booms over the loudspeaker. "If I catch that dog in this auditorium one more time, I'll disqualify your friends."

From backstage, we can't hear Shaggy's response, but soon the squeak of a door closing echoes across the room. I lean my head back against the rack of props and costumes we're sitting cross-legged at the foot of. I kind of wish Scooby was back here with us—a calming force.

"I could really use some of the special tea you used to

make us before performances," Luna says.

"Yeah," Dusk softly agrees, chewing on her drumstick.

I feel a rush of shame that my abandonment of magic has consequences for my friends, even though my special herbal tea was always more helpful for warming our vocal cords than warming fate in our favor. Still, I can't risk it. We would have suffered much worse than scratchy throats if I hadn't given Wicca up.

"So," Jordan says from her own trio also waiting to perform. "What's the theme of the Hex Girls? Are you supposed to be some sort of goth Destiny's Child?"

I tense and part my lips for a sharp retort, but Luna speaks up before I can start anything. "I'll take that as a compliment."

"It was meant as one," Jordan says in the same passive-aggressive tone she uses for everything she says to me. "I'm only trying to extend some hospitality to you all. Not everyone is out to get you." Maybe I'd believe her, if this wasn't the fifth time she'd given us some backhanded compliment in front of the talent show hopefuls. Complimenting my outfit by saying she wished dark colors didn't wash her out in the spotlights of performance halls. Asking if my vegan diet was a therapeutic regimen to improve the strength of my vocal cords.

Interestingly, this is the first time she's included the band as a whole in her taunting. Most of her comments have been designed to annoy me specifically. It's probably because Daphne worked quickly and *The Daily Babbler*'s feature on the Hex Girls came out this morning. I hope Jordan gets it out of her system soon. I'll take any level of petty as long as Dusk and Luna are able to feel welcome here.

Waiting feels like torture even without Jordan's unwanted company. We've watched act after act take the stage for their final auditions and heard applause and excited squeals as well as "I'm sorry, but no" and "Maybe next year!"

Jordan's band, Point Blank, is called ahead of ours. I don't know why she is so threatened by the Hex Girls—we sound nothing alike. Their sound is more pop than the goth punk rock vibe we aim for, and while our songs are about magic and the world around us, the original song they're singing now is about life around Coolsville. They're talented, I can admit that. It's not much of a surprise to hear happy sounds from the crowd soon after they finish. Jordan may be cruel, but she carries a mean tune too.

I have faith we'll make it, but I will feel better when we know for certain. It would take the edge off this nagging fear that things will start to unravel, like the sanctuary of the community garden did with all that gossip. I've switched my preferred shift times to before school to avoid working with either of those girls again.

But the suspicious things they said about my friends have stuck in my head. Not because I believe them, but because it worries me that even a group of people as kind and well-intentioned as Mystery Inc. could be so misunderstood. I don't want to know what they'd say about me if my past was discovered.

Or my more recent failure. The fall of the pioneer statue has thus far been interpreted as nothing more than the collapse of an aging monument in earthquake-prone California, but I can't risk anything else abnormal. Nothing spooky like that can happen again.

"The Hex Girls," the loudspeaker calls.

"Just like last time," Dusk says. I'm not sure if she's addressing the whole band or just herself. I follow her and Luna out into the spotlights. It's much more disorienting walking onstage from the wings rather than ascending from the crowd.

I count us down before my eyes have adjusted to the brightness. It works out better not to see anyone until we're deep into the song. By the time I can make out the figures before me, we've already found our groove.

We're not the only ones singing in unison on the final line this time. The Mystery Inc. gang joins in, of course, but more of the same crowd from the first day are also jamming along as we play. We actually have to wait a bit for the applause to finish before the judges can speak, which is validating all by itself.

The only thing I can hear is my own heartbeat as the judges discuss our fate.

"Thorn McKnight, Jane Brooks, and Kimberly Hale of the Hex Girls," the drama teacher—and chief judge—addresses us, "we would be delighted to have you join us in this year's Coolsville High talent show."

"Yes!" Dusk screams, leaping from the drum set to

gather Luna and me in a hug. I can't hear my own cheers over our mutual excitement. As we catch our breath, a new noise rises from the crowd, some kind of banging. I peek out of our group hug to see if Scooby has snuck back into the auditorium.

I'm not the only one looking for the source of the noise. The audience is no longer looking at us, and the judges are too distracted to either call the next act or boot us from the stage. The sound isn't inside the building.

Something is going on outside.

The series of thuds and clangs grows louder and then— unmistakably—a scream.

Several students retreat farther into the theater, but Shaggy yells, "Scooby's out there!" and that's all it takes to send the gang running *toward* the exit.

The arms of my best friends fall from my shoulders. We share a look, then follow Mystery Inc. But none of us are prepared for what prompted the scream.

Today's assigned student gardeners cower in fear in the dirt like startled pill bugs. Shovels and rakes—all so mindfully organized when I finished my last shift—lie forgotten in a heap, barely visible in the haze rising from the ground. At first, I don't understand what has the gardeners so afraid, nor why Scooby is pushing against Shaggy's legs like he wants them to leave the garden despite the wealth of unprotected vegetables that he could be snacking on.

Then I realize the fog obscuring the garden tools is moving. Rapidly, and with purpose.

Like it's *alive*.

Hovering above the garden is a being made of mist, but not the picturesque mist of a morning fog in autumn. This mist is a toxic neon green. Its face is as indistinct as the rest of its body. Two cavernous gaps undulate where eyes should be, like black holes seeking to swallow anything in their path.

The mouth, a similar ominous abyss, contorts into a sickening distended grin.

"My dearest Hex Girls, I am your humble host." It greets us with a deep voice that echoes across the courtyard.

"What?" I ask, the word exhaled in shock so quietly no one can hear it above the screams around us. "Our . . . host?" I repeat, dumbfounded. I've never seen this creature or anything like it before.

"I'm so very much looking forward to all we'll do together," it says, unfazed by our lack of recognition. "I'll see you again soon. But in the meantime, I hope you like my welcome present."

Suddenly, it dives toward us. I crouch to take cover and hear thuds and more screaming as those around me do the same, but nothing else follows.

And just like that, the mist creature is gone. I spin around, looking in all directions, but it's disappeared.

"Are you okay?" Fred asks the gardeners, who I now recognize as Kailey and the boy from the first day. Kailey takes Fred's offered hand to climb to her feet, despite all the mean things she had to say about him the other day.

"I think so," she says, sounding shaken up. "It came out of nowhere. There was no warning." She says this last part with a pointed look at me.

I don't know what explanation she expects out of me. The mist monster has left nothing behind except a matching fog that continues to rise from a green dust on the plants. Kailey loses her balance again and steps backward on what was once a healthy plant. It crumbles to mush beneath her shoe.

That's when I look around again and notice that the entire garden is covered in the same green residue, and that every plant it touches is mutating. The fresh harvest is rotting right before our eyes.

In moments, everything is destroyed.

CHAPTER NINE

The crowd is as unruly as a mosh pit by the time the police arrive. Kailey and the other student gardener sit under foil blankets next to the destruction of all their hard work, coughing a bit from the green fog they inhaled. Just yesterday my hands were in that soil, and now everything is dead. The fog over the garden has faded, but some faint tendrils remain, a reminder that this wasn't a dream.

It's a living nightmare, and I'm the star.

At least, that's the consensus poisoning the minds of the

students around me. Rumors are already becoming as toxic as the mist, a game of telephone I desperately want to cut short. Being blamed for the statue would have been better, since I was actually there when that happened.

Fingers point and then drop away when I catch their owners' eyes. I'm sure they all have the exact same question, one that my bandmates and I also have, though no one has the courage to voice it out loud. It doesn't matter what that *thing* said. This can't be my fault.

I would never spawn something so cruel and destructive. Not intentionally, at least.

Luna locks her hand in Dusk's as we wait to give our statements. Even though that creature addressed the band as a whole, the two of them have inched away from me so subtly I'm not sure they're even aware they did so.

There's an invisible circle around me, marking me off-limits to normal people.

The cops have their hands full sorting the actual witnesses from those who arrived after. Most of the other callback acts retreated deeper into the auditorium when the commotion started, but once the immediate danger of the mist monster disappeared, the garden suddenly became a *very* interesting attraction.

In addition to the rest of the callback acts, the crowd around the unfurled yellow tape contains athletes finishing up practice and other students still on campus for after-school activities. Parents are pulling into the parking lot at the edge of campus, curious about the giant crowd of teens.

There's only one car slowly pulling *out* of the lot instead of into it. I can't see the driver from this distance, but I don't need to. If the paint job wasn't obvious, the bright orange of Velma's cardigan racing toward it would be answer enough. I watch as Velma shakes something off her fingers, hands Daphne a beaker, and then accepts Shaggy's hand to pull her inside the van. I didn't notice the gang slipping away earlier, but I certainly can't blame them for it.

Standing within the border of the squared-off garden makes me feel more like an exhibit than a victim. Can I really even call myself a victim? The mist, both sentient and sulfuric, never touched me. The girls and I never left the covered walkway outside the theater entrance. We could have escaped unconnected to what happened, if not for that direct callout.

Maybe that's why the gang didn't warn us they were leaving. They knew we didn't have any choice but to stay. We're a part of this, but I don't know why. It can't be connected to Oakhaven. Sarah and Ben Ravencroft are gone. Trapped. Dead, if that fire did its job.

"I swear," Kailey pleads with the cop interviewing her, "it was *alive.*"

The cop, who's not much older than we are, probably barely out of the academy, shakes his head. "No, ma'am. You're mistaken."

An older officer shoulders past me to address the students loitering at the edge of the crime scene tape. "There is nothing to see here," he says in a booming, smoke-aged voice. "I recognize faces in this crowd, so if you don't want me to start calling your parents to tell them you're interfering with official police business I suggest you clear out." The threat works pretty efficiently at thinning the herd, leaving only the gardeners and my band to interrogate.

A woman who is obviously Kailey's mother rushes past the tape, her cross-body purse fluttering like a cape behind her. The younger officer releases her daughter and the other student gardener to her custody. He moves on to my friends as a duo, united without me. Luna and Dusk keep glancing guiltily at me as they recount their version of events, though they work hard not to single me out.

But they should.

I don't know why that *thing* addressed the Hex Girls, but it has to have something to do with me. I was the only one of us who had anything to do with the garden. The older officer seems to agree. As he approaches me, he holds a hand up to stop the younger officer from following him. "Ms. McKnight, correct?" he asks.

My fingers scratch nervously at my palms. "Yes," I say. "That's me."

"I'm Sheriff Jones of the Coolsville Police Department," he says. His eyes narrow as he studies me, not even trying to hide the suspicion in them. "I'd like to hear what *you* think happened here today." He chooses each word carefully, seeming to make the sentence as a whole perfectly above board and normal on paper. But this isn't a written report. The tone of his voice and the specific word he emphasizes in his otherwise harmless statements imply an entirely different conversation to be had.

"I saw what everyone else did," I tell him, as carefully and as calmly as I can manage. "I was in the auditorium when I heard a scream, so I came outside."

"Why?" the sheriff asks. I don't reply immediately, mostly because I'm not sure what he means. He lets out a big, impatient sigh, like my bafflement is typical, but annoying. "Why did you leave the building if you thought something bad might have happened outside?"

"Because someone could have been hurt," I say. It's less sarcastic than *because I saw my friends go first*, though Velma and the others were the first out the door. I honestly can't say I was really thinking about anything concrete in the moment. It wasn't a choice I had time to deliberate on, but if I had, I still would have gone to help.

"You're sticking with that answer?" Sheriff Jones presses.

I look past him to the girls, who are still sharing their own story with the rookie. "Yes," I say, my eyes on them, "it's the truth."

"Ms. McKnight," Sheriff Jones says, "we are discussing something serious here. Please keep your attention on me when I am speaking to you."

"I'm sorry," I say, then regret it when the corners of his mouth tip up slightly below his dirty-blond mustache. Is he glad I'm embarrassed? Was it his intention to trap me? I don't feel in control or confident in my answers anymore, even though I know what I saw. "I followed my friends," I confess. "They left first. The girls and I followed them."

"The girls?"

"My bandmates," I say. "They're talking to the other officer. Right over there." I point. "That's who I was looking at. I'm sorry."

"That's fine," the sheriff says. He jots something down on a notepad I didn't see him pull out. "It's been an eventful afternoon. People get distracted. Confused." I nod. "Who were your other friends? The ones who left first?"

"One of them is Fred Jones. Maybe he's your nephew?" I offer optimistically, but the complete erasure of the tiny glee Sheriff Jones gained from reprimanding me tells me otherwise. Fred is definitely related to him, but not as distantly as I would prefer. That is the disappointment of a father glaring at me.

"Let's move past that," he says gruffly, though I feel like a proper report would want me to clarify on the record that Fred was indeed accompanied by who we both know he was. "What did you see when you exited the theater?"

I tell him about the cowered gardeners and then describe the thing inside the mist to the best of my ability, but he interrupts me to critique my choice of words. "There are no such things as monsters," he says.

"I don't know how else to describe it." *I don't want it to be a monster either, Sheriff Jones.* I've had enough of those for a lifetime, but what else could it be?

He writes more on his notepad. "The student gardeners informed me you attended a volunteer shift earlier this week.

Signed up for it pretty last minute, too."

"Yes," I say. "I'm new here and I signed up as soon as I heard about the garden, on my first day of school. I don't know what that has to do with any of this."

"I think your actions, your *choices*," he emphasizes, "since you've arrived here could contain all the answers to today's events, Ms. McKnight. Rather than blame misdeeds on monsters that don't exist, I think we should focus instead on the factors that have roots in provable facts. This whole thing looks like a mean-spirited prank to me."

"A prank," I repeat.

"Indeed," Sheriff Jones says. He smirks and crosses his arms, clearly taking joy in revealing his big theory. "Let's say a teenage girl with an affinity for counterculture and disruption"—his eyes scan me as he speaks, lingering with growing disapproval on each successive item of dark clothing—"moves to a new town and seeks to make a memorable impression on her new classmates. What better way to do so than stage a theatrical moment to advertise her band somewhere she both had prior access to and could ensure a sizable audience?"

"You think I did this as a prank?" I ask. A small of part of me manages to be shocked, which is almost more surprising than being accused. It's not like I'm not used to being judged by others, especially authoritative adults. "Wouldn't it make equal sense to say this was a prank played *on me*?"

"This was a destructive act. It was meant to leave a lasting reminder." Sheriff Jones gestures to the ruined garden. "Like you said, you've only been here for a few days. That doesn't give anyone else much time to know you well enough to target you."

"Except your son," I say. Though I would sooner say I did it than believe any of Mystery Inc. was responsible, I have a feeling that bringing up Fred is the best way to end a conversation with the sheriff. "I've known your son and his friends for a while now. I'm sure he's mentioned that. People here know it. You can ask the girl who told you about my shift. Kailey, right? She saw Fred here, too. He helped her up after the incident."

Sheriff Jones's pen hand stills on the notepad, and his eyes thin into slits.

"Should I slow down?" I ask politely, smiling at him. If he wants a well-behaved girl, I'll give him one. A good girl wouldn't hide any important details, would she? "I can repeat myself if you'd like to write this down too."

"I don't think that will be necessary," he says. "The evidence doesn't really point to Fred being involved in any way."

Fred Jones uses his connections to get them out of trouble, Kailey had said. Here's a connection standing before me. But it doesn't really seem like Fred is the one intentionally trying to avoid an official paper trail. If he had felt confident that his presence would stay off the record, why would the gang flee before the cops arrived?

"The evidence doesn't really point to me being responsible either," I say. "If you consider the details of my *full* statement. I can come to the station with my father, if you need me to."

"No, this will be fine for now," he says. He shuts his notepad and slides it into a pocket on his multipurpose belt. "I think it best that you keep your head down and stick to your studies going forward, Ms. McKnight, no matter the intended target of this . . . misdeed. You shouldn't seek trouble for the sake of it."

"I promise you, I won't."

CHAPTER TEN

I can't believe that my biggest stressor at the start of the week was the humiliation of introducing myself to my new classmates over and over again. What I wouldn't give to redo it all. I'd face the nerves of being a fresh face a thousand times over if it would erase the impression Coolsville High has of me now.

The longer I stare at the wilting lettuce on my fork, the deeper my appetite retreats. I can see what's left of the garden from our lunch table in the middle of the courtyard.

The edge of the garden peeks out just past the sciences building, far enough that the odor of decayed and rotted plants doesn't carry, but the shame does.

The Harvest Host, as the gossip mill has termed the specter in the mist, is a weight on my shoulders. Gone is any goodwill from our first days here, all the curiosity that came with being new in town mutated like the crops into a suffocating cloud of suspicion.

"Eat something, Thorn," Luna encourages, but her concern only dampens my hunger further. She shouldn't be worrying about me when her reputation is on the line too.

I shake my head and drop my fork back into the plastic container on the sun-bleached table. "I'm distracted," I say, trying to keep my voice light. "I'm not used to eating outside yet, that's all."

"You'll get the hang of it," Shaggy says around a mouthful of sandwich. "Does that mean you're not gonna finish that?"

I push my nearly untouched salad toward him. He eagerly takes the top piece of bread off what's left of his sandwich and piles the lettuce onto it. I hand him my unopened pouch of dressing, which he glazes the top with. It's the least I can do to thank the gang for their unwavering loyalty despite the shifting tide of public opinion. Despite leaving me to face Fred's father alone yesterday, they still pushed a second table against their regular one to save a spot for me and the girls at lunch today. Just like they did yesterday and the day before. The host's claim hasn't changed anything in their eyes. I think it's even endeared us to them more.

"Don't worry, Thorn," Fred says. He's also ignoring his lunch, but not out of anxiety like I am. He's busy copying something from a search result on his phone onto a notepad that looks strikingly similar to the one his father was holding yesterday. The cover rests half folded against his sports drink, the police department logo almost fully obscured by stickers.

Earlier today, I asked him about his dad's aggressive eagerness to blame yesterday's disaster on teen mischief. I made it a point *not* to mention the rumors about keeping his record clean, but that didn't make a difference. Even without directly mentioning the gossip I didn't believe, he was visibly upset by his father's lack of interest in investigating anything abnormal.

"We'll stop that mist monster," he promises without looking up from his notes.

"And prove your innocence," Velma adds.

My innocence. Not the Hex Girls'. I drop my chin into my hands, both relieved and frustrated it's so obvious to everyone that this unwanted connection is to me and me alone. I want my bandmates as far from this as possible, but this is the second time Mystery Inc.'s investigative skills have isolated me in a case.

This is different, though. It has to be. The Ravencrofts are gone. They can't have followed me here. It's impossible.

I can still feel the weight of Sarah's spell book in my hands, my voice shaking as I spoke the words that Velma insisted only I was capable of using to save everyone. My town, my best friends, my father—everything and everyone I loved in danger.

"How exactly are you going to do that?" I ask her. I was up all night thinking about what had happened, breaking it apart, rewinding and replaying everything I remembered to try to uncover anything that made any sense. If it had been a prank, like Sheriff Jones suggested, there was no clear calling card.

I stared at those ruined crops before the authorities arrived. I can still see them every time I close my eyes.

"I gathered some of the soil to run an experiment," Velma says. I flash back to the beaker she'd handed Daphne before they all fled. I expect her to explain, but instead she changes the subject. "Do you want some of my tamales? They're vegetarian."

"No," I say, "but thank you for offering."

"I'll try one," Dusk says. I'm the only one of the three of us who's made the full leap to veganism so far.

Velma folds a napkin around a tamale with one hand and lightly slaps at Shaggy's outstretched palm with the other. "I already gave you one!" she scolds him. "Thorn," she says to me, "please don't worry. There could be a rational explanation for all this."

"There usually is," Daphne agrees. Fred looks up at her from his notepad, mouth half open as if he planned to comment but thought better of it. "Most of the time, anyway," she amends.

I know I can trust my friends to get to the bottom of this

mystery. That's how I met them in the first place, after all. I didn't know what to think when I first crossed paths with Mystery Inc., and the feeling was mutual. A group of friends so loyal that they decided to go into business together, despite their age, was relatable to me. Dusk, Luna, and I had formed the Hex Girls when we were twelve. But I didn't understand the gang's insistence on poking their heads into stuff that didn't concern them, especially when I was their initial suspect.

It wasn't until the danger escalated and they stayed to fix things despite their fear that my feelings changed. They had no obligation to protect Oakhaven. They had no duty to save us from the Ravencrofts. They did it because it was the right thing to do.

That's how I know that they'll see this through too. Mystery Inc. has never met a question they didn't want answered. I know I should be grateful they're on my side, but I came to Coolsville to escape the aftermath of their time in Oakhaven. I don't want to flee another town.

"Do you think it's going to show up again?" a voice asks a few tables from ours. There's no need to clarify what they're talking about.

"I wouldn't be the person to ask about that," Jordan replies. She's sitting on top of a table in the fractured shade of a thin tree, waving a chip bag like it's a conductor's wand. "I was only a witness," she says to the small but growing crowd. "The Harvest Host didn't name *me*."

"She wasn't even there," I mutter bitterly.

"It'll be fine," Luna says. "She just wants attention."

I look to Dusk for backup, but she has nothing to say. She's tearing the napkin from her finished tamale into tiny little pieces. She won't even look at Jordan. It's not like her. Dusk's temper is super short. She's usually the first of us to stand up if someone is being cruel to anyone she cares about, but she's been so restrained since we moved.

I think she's holding back because of me.

This is all my fault. I dragged them away from their entire life only to force them back into guilt by association. It's not fair. I step out of the bench seat.

"Thorn," Luna tries, but I'm already walking away.

"No, it didn't name you," I agree with Jordan as I arrive at her table. "Because you weren't in the garden yesterday. You left the auditions before it arrived. *Right* before it showed up, if I remember correctly."

Jordan scoffs. "Like your version of events is trustworthy." She rolls her eyes, unfazed at being called out in a lie.

"The police said they were looking at this as a prank," I say. "If I had to throw out names of who could be cruel enough to do something like that, yours sounds about right."

Jordan hops down from her table. "So funny you should bring up names," she says, sauntering toward me. I walk backward as she gains on me. "Isn't it, *Sally*?"

I stop moving.

"I don't know about the rest of you," Jordan says, glancing theatrically around at the growing crowd of onlookers, "but I find it really interesting how 'Thorn' here is the only

90

member of her band so insistent on being addressed solely by her stage name."

"You're Kimberly, right?" She turns to address Luna, who finally gives up her pacifism to glare at her. "I heard Jane's name in roll call." She gestures lazily at Dusk. "That's what sparked my curiosity. It made me wonder why you were so secretive about your own name. So I looked you up."

No, no, no. I back farther away from Jordan's small but sinister frame, hoping she'll leave me alone if I leave her alone. She doesn't stop talking, though. "If you look up Thorn McKnight online, you'll only find articles about the Hex Girls or plants. But if you search her real name, the results are far more interesting. You should all try it," she suggests. "Type in 'Sally McKnight.'"

I watch as my classmates do just that, phone screens glowing bright and as toxic as the mist.

"An evil witch?" someone gasps. "She burned half the town down."

A finger points at me. "She's destroyed things before," the accuser adds, shoving their screen in the face of another. "She performed magic with another witch."

"That's not—" I start, but my defense dies in my throat. They won't believe what actually happened. Not now.

"I heard you were really eager to work in the garden," Jordan says. She looks me dead in the eye as she adds, "You were there before the host arrived, weren't you?"

Confirmations swirl around me as students trade stories about Oakhaven, looking at me suspiciously.

"The whole town was set on fire."

"What's that about her father?"

"Of course that's how she knows those four—can't believe they invited her here."

I flee the courtyard.

CHAPTER ELEVEN

Jordan's hateful laugh follows me far longer than it should, ringing in my ears like tinnitus even as I settle in the library. The silence of the space only emphasizes the echo of her jeers. As I wander into the fiction section, it still feels like monsters linger around me, pressing at my back in the aisle where I've sunk down to hide from the wandering librarian.

I stay put after the ending lunch bells sound across campus, even as the guilt makes my stomach churn. It's almost laughable that for all my edgy goth persona, I've never done something as intentionally rebellious as skipping class before.

So much of my life is a cruel joke now. Singing about enchanting an audience when I can't even bring myself to brew an herbal tea of goodwill. My chosen wardrobe implying that I don't care about the only thing I fear nowadays: unwanted attention.

I wish monsters had stayed in the pages of books. My life was simpler when evil witches were just an ill-advised tourist attraction. When ghosts were just decorations that dotted the streets in October. Less than a year ago, I would have been as certain as Sheriff Jones that the Harvest Host was nothing more than a onetime prank. My concern would be solely focused on the wreckage of the garden, not where the mist monster might manifest next.

I'd give anything to return to the days when dark things intrigued me instead of defined me. It's clear now that Luna was right. I'm never going to be able to outrun what happened in Oakhaven.

But this is the worst possible way for my classmates to learn the truth.

Soft footfalls shuffle toward me from a few aisles away. I scurry back as quietly as I can, crawling with no clear direction except escape. I stop with rug burn on my palms and knees in a far corner. The shadows are longer here and the books covered in dust, which makes sense once I rise up a little to read the label for this section: LOCAL HISTORY.

Oakhaven had leaned too heavily into the stories of our

ancestors, a lesson we learned the hard way. There wasn't much else to do in a town so small. Colonial reenactments only attract so many road-tripping families and nerdy academics. Coolsville has much more to entice visitors. Proximity to a beach probably brings Coolsville twice Oakhaven's entire yearly tourism revenue in the summer months alone.

It's clear that this section of the library is more for the town's ego than anything else. The same books number in the dozens; they're probably only ever checked out for class assignments. There aren't as many windows over here—which suits me just fine—to protect the small artifacts on display, like a print too pristine to be the original town charter and some chipped remnants of fake gold nuggets above books about the long-closed mines.

The centerpiece of the mini-exhibit is a near-life-size portrait of people I assume must be the town founders. A white couple in stereotypical pioneer garb, the same ones who were depicted in the toppled statue. They wear near-opposite expressions. It's an odd tribute in several respects. The first thing that stands out is that it's a photo, not a painting, but that only surprises me as a New England girl since the American East Coast was established so much earlier than towns out here. Still, most old ceremonial photos I've seen look more . . . well, ceremonial.

The photo was taken outside instead of in a controlled studio setup. The man sits on a large rock, with the woman standing next to him. The man's eyes are so haunted that

95

I can't tell if he's as old as he looks or prematurely aged by grief. He's dressed like he's well-off, but that doesn't really reveal much about his past. Many formerly destitute people became rich overnight in gold rush towns.

The woman next to him appears to contain every ounce of happiness he lacks. She looks at him instead of the camera, smiling calmly. Her hair is only half up, which seems at odds with the trends of the time, but it's not the sole fashion faux pax. Both of them are dressed like they only posed for the photo as a last-minute decision, with bandannas tied around their necks and a hat to ward off the sun resting politely in the lap of the man. They look like they have better things to do than sit for a photo for as long as one took back then.

Below them, a plaque reads THE TIME FOR FEAR IS OVER. SERENITY IS THE ONLY SOLUTION FOR COOLSVILLE. —LEVI AND LAURA COOLIDGE, 1849

Yikes. That's a much creepier way to say *Everything's chill in Coolsville*. No wonder the town motto was updated at some point.

"They would have hated you," Velma says. I jump, clenching my teeth to stop the yelp of surprise as she appears at my side. I don't know how she knew where to find me. Maybe she wasn't even looking for me at all. She has several books tucked under her arm to check out, reminding me that a library is not an unlikely place to run into Velma Dinkley.

"Yeah?" I ask mindlessly, still taking in her sudden appearance instead of her words.

"They were all about things staying the same. Staying boring. And you and the Hex Girls are the most interesting thing to happen to Coolsville in a long time," Velma says to the portrait. She says it like it's a good thing. Her grin almost matches Laura Coolidge's, sure and steadfast, but her happiness doesn't reach her eyes. She flicks those brown irises toward me. "You and the specter," she adds.

I sink back down to the floor, no strength left in me after Jordan's ambush. I have no idea how I'll get out of this. How I'll get my *friends* out of this. Dusk and Luna gave up everything for me once already. I can't force them to do it again.

"Everyone knows." I state the obvious. I tuck my head in the gap between my bent knees, my long red-black hair shielding my face like a closing act curtain.

I feel Velma settle next to me and set her books down. Her kitten heels tuck in under the pleats of her skirt, barely visible through the breaks in my hair curtain. That tiny rebellion against her short stature, as if a half-inch boost will make a difference to her four-foot-nine frame, is so at odds with her logical acceptance of most things that I can't help but smile.

She's so softly feminine. It's all I can think about as I watch her hand, nails painted in sunset colors, lightly take mine in that small window of vision below my hair. Her thumb rubs reassurance into my palm. I think, *Do you do your own nails? Or does Daphne do them for you?* It's a safer train of thought than the more pressing issue of the day, because this train can't go anywhere. *Did you pair thigh-high socks with that short skirt to cover your legs or to draw attention to them?* is another perfectly safe question because it will never be asked.

I lift my head to look at her directly. It's not much safer to look into her eyes than to hide in the dark. Her kind brown eyes are just as dangerous as our clasped hands. Maybe even more so. I'm already lost in the landscape of one ruination. And yet here I am, risking another, the classic trap of falling for a friend. One who has only tried to help me out of kindness. Who I'm not even sure would be interested in dating me.

While I'm lost in my thoughts, Velma lets go of my hand. I blink back the irrational rush of sadness.

"We're going to fix this," Velma says, determined. *Not possible*, I think. She leans away from me and reaches for her stack of books, rearranging them until she's unearthed the one she wants. I lower my knees a little for a better view. I immediately regret it.

Wicca: A Beginner's History, the cover reads.

"I picked this one for you," she says.

"I don't want it," I say, but I don't stop my traitorous hands from taking the book as she holds it out to me, even as my heart races at the touch of its weathered, creased cover.

"You did," Velma reminds me, "before."

I shake my head, even though I know it's true. When we became pen pals I was still in shock over the role magic had played in defeating the Ravencrofts. My magic in particular.

I wanted to know more. All I'd known about Wicca was fragments of traditions Dad remembered from back when my mother was alive. I told Velma about my feelings then, but those were the early days.

Before magic's presence in my life soured from a connection to the earth and the memory of my mother into the reason no one in town would look me in the eye anymore. Before I went from being a Wiccan to being a *witch*. Before things got so bad in my hometown I had to leave everything behind, magic being the least of the sacrifices I had to make.

"You should put it back on the shelf," I say. I try to give the book back to Velma, but she refuses.

"I can't," she says. "I didn't get it here. I bought it an occult store outside of town."

"You didn't have to do that for me." *You really shouldn't have.* "Thank you," I concede, sliding the book from my lap to my bag with a single finger, like prolonged exposure could infect me. "How did you know to find me here?"

"I didn't," she admits. She opens one of the books and lifts a hall pass. "I tutor during this hour and came here for reference material."

"Oh," I say, hoping my face doesn't betray my disappointment that this was just a coincidence.

"I'll walk back with you to class, if you'd like?" she says. "I assume you don't have one of these." She waves the hall pass.

"No, I don't."

She offers the same hand she held mine with to help me

up. I take it and follow her, not quite relieved but feeling less hopeless after our talk. As we walk through the library, I'm silent, as our surroundings demand, but Velma keeps laughing under her breath.

"What?" I ask.

"Nothing," she tries, but her voice cracks on the single word. "It's just . . . You saw that Coolidge quote. Did you really think the Coolsville High library would carry books encouraging witchcraft?"

CHAPTER TWELVE

The next few days are more of the same. My pink bedroom becomes a sanctuary I never expected, especially as I cover up the color by putting pictures and vintage band posters on the walls. I have to make it more appealing, because the only joy to be found in Coolsville for me now is at home.

I know stories are spreading through neighborhood watch groups, because Dad has stopped telling me about how his day went, even though that was the only effective path he's had to starting a conversation with me lately. It seems like his past has been unearthed too. The only difference is that he deserves the judgment for what he did.

Adults don't stoop to taunting or mocking me to my face. Most simply give me disapproving looks, which isn't unusual given I dress like I have a funeral to attend every day. But I know they're for a different reason this time. Parents like to pretend they are above what their children are doing to each other, but they are equally prone to gossip.

It's these types of looks that follow me in the nursery today as Luna, Dusk, and I shop for a sibling to join my Venus flytrap in the pink dungeon. I try to shrug the looks off, but the judgmental glares hit differently in a place like this, where I'm surrounded by plants. I can picture myself as others must see me, a monster as menacing as the specter in the mist. A witch as devious as Sarah Ravencroft, hungry only for destruction.

Even in my dreams I can't remember anymore what Oakhaven looked like before her return. The scorched remains of my hometown are the only backdrop my mind can conjure, awake or unconscious. It's nothing but flames and soot, even when Sarah doesn't feature in my nightmares. I'm nothing like her. I'm an environmentalist. An eco-goth. I love nature.

Sarah never loved anything. She only cared about power.

The last thing I would ever want to do is hurt anybody, especially by destroying plants. Not that the owner of the nursery would believe me. He's been watching me from the counter since we set foot in the store, even though there's a salesman in front of him who is trying very hard to claim his attention instead.

"GreenGrove is more than just landscaping," I hear the salesman say. "We pair gardening care with the innovative possibilities of tech." The owner nods along, his eyes glued to me as I investigate a bulb-shaped succulent.

The salesman rambles on. "How much time do you spend watering and fertilizing your nursery? I could implant smart monitors in your plant beds that constantly track the health of your entire inventory, even when you sleep. I could do it today."

I pick up a decorative pot from an open-ended shelf. It's handmade, shaped and painted to resemble a dark green cactus. The thorns are softer than they look; the subtle strokes make the many small knots appear a lot sharper than they are. I bounce the pot in my hands for a moment, catching Luna's eye as I pretend it's pricking me. She laughs lightly, distracted from the seed packets she's been looking at.

Dusk doesn't join in. Her eyes are narrowed in the direction that mine just left. I'm not shocked to see the shopkeeper still watching me instead of the man trying to sell him something. I look back at Dusk and smirk before tossing the decorative pot again, higher this time. I do it a few times. The pot is airborne for a fraction of second at most, always landing safely back in my hands.

But it pisses the shopkeeper off. He huffs from behind the counter. Dusk finally smiles.

"You can inspect each plant individually on a tablet

like this with our app," the salesman goes on. "And if you really want to save money, you could eliminate a full-time employee with our automated watering drones. That could save you thousands in the first year alone."

The mention of money intrigues the shopkeeper. The salesman finally has his full attention, which means the shopkeeper is thankfully done staring at me. The two of them peruse the options displayed on the branded tablet the salesman brought with him. The shopkeeper only checks on us once or twice more.

"Are you guys getting anything?" I ask.

Luna shakes her head, putting the seed packets back where she found them. "I think there are better places to spend our money," she says with a nod toward the men.

"I agree," I say.

"Then we might as well leave," Dusk says. "I can't take much more of Mr. Turn-Nature-into-an-App over there." The GreenGrove salesman doesn't miss a beat in his spiel, even though Dusk definitely spoke loud enough for him to hear. She heads toward the door like the decision has already been made. We follow her, not missing the tension ease from the shopkeeper's creased brow.

"Wait for us!" Luna jokes, raising a hand in salute to shield her face from the late-afternoon sun once we get outside. Dusk rolls her eyes. She knows she can't go anywhere without us. Or at least, she's not supposed to. We all took the same bus here from school, and Mystery Inc. is going to pick us up at six.

"Are we still going apple picking?" I ask. We usually have band practice three nights a week, but tonight Daphne has invited us to join the gang at a local orchard.

"You promised them we would," Dusk says. She doesn't sound too enthused about it, but it's not like the three of us have received many other social invitations since the arrival of the Harvest Host.

I sit on the curb and resist the urge to pick at the premade tears in my distressed jeans. Luna joins me, but Dusk remains standing, watching the empty street like a concerned parent surveys the clouds for a storm front rolling in. "You're looking forward to it, right?" I ask Luna in a whisper.

"I am," she answers at a normal volume. "I think it will be nice to go to the orchard. But . . ."

"But . . ." I prompt after her pause.

"You could have asked us before committing to it," Dusk finishes for her.

Luna nods. Her nose squishes up, like it always does when she's forced to admit something she doesn't want to. As if telling a bitter truth tastes like it feels to hear.

"I'm sorry," I say. "I just thought it would be a nice distraction. I thought you liked the gang. You guys do like them, right?" I hadn't even considered the possibility of my two friend groups being at odds with each other. They hadn't spent much time together in Oakhaven, but it seemed like everyone got along there . . . once we were cleared as suspects.

"They're your friends, not mine," Dusk says. She doesn't say anything else for a moment, then adds, "I like the dog, though. He's nice."

"I think they're great," Luna says, and even though she's a peacemaker at heart, I know she's being genuine. "I'm really enjoying getting to know Fred. He has lots of subscriptions to engineering magazines and websites. You know I'm considering majoring in engineering, so it's been fun to have someone to talk about it with."

"That's good," I say, more to myself than to Luna.

Dusk crosses her arms and looks down at me, her lips scrunched to one side. "Daphne got me a hookup at the thrift shop for some new clothes," she says, somewhat reluctantly. "It was a pretty good selection for a recommendation from such a preppy girl."

"So it's not all bad," I say. Dusk nods. She lowers herself to the curb and sits next to Luna, leaving me at the end of the line.

I take up the watch she abandoned on the empty street, waiting for the Mystery Machine to make its appearance. My best friends converse lightly about the plants in the shop and I nod and agree when appropriate, trying to believe that I'm not fracturing *all* my relationships.

CHAPTER THIRTEEN

It's a cramped ride to the orchard with seven people and a giant dog, but spirits get higher when we arrive and see the fresh twilight glow on the treetops.

Dusk takes off with Scooby and Shaggy for a game of catch with some of the fallen apples as soon as the van's back doors open, and Luna joins Daphne to gather apple-picking baskets, which leaves me with the most inquisitive members of the group. Velma, perhaps sensing my discomfort, doesn't say anything as we exit the Mystery Machine. But

Fred is already taking in the greenery with a tactical eye and reaching back into the van.

He's pulling out ropes, nets, baskets . . . things that seem like they could be used to build a trap.

Wait.

"Do you think the Harvest Host is going to show up here tonight?" I ask, trying to sound casual instead of terrified. I didn't even consider that possibility, though I really should have.

"No," Velma says, at the same time Fred admits, "Maybe."

"It's probably not going to show up tonight," Velma says, "but it's better to be safe than sorry."

"The main goal is to pick enough apples to have some left for pies after Shaggy starts eating them on the way home," Fred jokes. "I promise you, Thorn, the Harvest Host is not why we invited you here tonight. I just wanted to be ready in case it did."

I nod like it's no big deal and lean against the brightly painted Mystery Machine to keep myself from pacing with anxiety while we wait for Luna and Daphne to return with the baskets. Velma waits with me and mercifully doesn't say anything more about the host.

"Hey, Fred, I have a question for you," Luna says when she and Daphne get back.

"Go for it," he says. He starts loading the thin ropes into one of the baskets and puts a net in another. Velma steps forward to pick up an empty basket before returning to me. I give her a genuine smile, relieved that this silent action confirms that at least two of us don't have to be on monster duty tonight.

"If the Harvest Host is a monster made of mist," Luna says, "how exactly do you plan to catch it with a physical trap?"

Daphne guffaws, doubling over from the strength of her laughter. The others join in as Fred attempts to explain his reasoning. "Come on, guys!" he shouts over the giggling. "This is serious."

"I'm sorry," Luna says, still snorting a little. "Go on."

"Okay, so," he says, reaching into the basket with the net, "we think the monster is made of mist, but to be sure, I have this small makeshift catapult—"

"Ignoring the mist issue," I interrupt, "do you have any other suspects? Or ideas?" I'm begging for any explanation other than magic and monsters.

"Yes, we do!" Daphne says, almost too excitedly. "That girl from the tryouts. The mean one?"

"Jordan?" I ask. I look to see if Dusk overheard Daphne accusing her new friend, but she's still busy playing fetch with Scooby and Shaggy.

"Yes," Daphne confirms. "I've been making a list of people who don't like you. It's pretty short, though, for what it's worth."

"The host might have nothing to do with you," Velma reminds me. "You could simply be a scapegoat. We're investigating that angle too."

"Great," I say, far more bitterly than I intend. "I mean,

109

that's good. I'm glad you're looking into different possibilities. I didn't do this. That *thing* . . . it isn't mine."

"We know that, Thorn," Fred says. "We're gonna catch whoever is doing this."

"Or whatever it is," Luna adds, twirling some of the rope in her basket. "With Fred's physics-defying trapping skills."

Fred grabs the spinning rope, accidentally starting a game of tug-of-war. "When you said you wanted to help," he says, grunting as he pulls against Luna's surprisingly firm grip, "I imagined a lot less sarcasm."

"That's okay," Luna says. "You don't know me that well yet. You'll learn."

Daphne follows the two of them as they drag each other in opposite directions. "If this is going to be a real battle, you need a proper referee," she says. "First one to fall is out." Right after she says this, Fred loses his footing in a small puddle of mud and nearly face-plants in the grass.

"Best out of three!" he shouts immediately. The chaos is entertaining enough to lure Shaggy, Scooby, and Dusk back from the edge of the orchard. Dusk calls dibs on replacing the next person to fall. Scooby creates an additional obstacle to conquer, crisscrossing underneath the rope stretched between Fred and Luna.

I'm the sole buzzkill, my positive mood totally ruined after mention of the host, so I try to step away unnoticed before I bring everyone else down with me.

CHAPTER FOURTEEN

"Thorn!" Velma calls after me just as I reach the tree line. I keep walking without looking back, but I slow my pace. She eventually catches up with me deep in the shade of the orchard. "I promise you we didn't invite you and the other Hex Girls out here as bait."

"I know," I say. But if it works out that way...

"There are a lot of places the host could target," she says, her apologetic tone morphing into something more assured and data driven. "If it even appears again. There's the nursery we picked you up from, the pumpkin patch, two parks, and some private farms." She lists the options methodically, no trace of fear or apprehension in her tone. I have no doubt she's gone over these options several times already, so I try to ignore the part of me that wants to ask if this lineup is in order of most to least likely.

I reach up to pick an apple. I grip it in my palm and spin it counterclockwise until it pops from the branch with the stem intact; then I bring it down and place it in the basket hooked on Velma's arm. I start for another, but she catches my arm before I can reach high enough. "Wow," she says. "You're a natural at this."

"Apple picking was a pretty common activity in Oakhaven," I explain. "It was really popular with the tourists seeking colonial reenactments. I used to pick up a few shifts at the local orchard guiding visitors through the process. There's a proper way to do it so you don't ruin your haul or damage the tree's ability to produce fruit again next year." I pick another apple, resting it softly next to the first in the basket. "It's important to me to protect the trees."

"Thorn," Velma says quietly, as if she's followed my spiraling train of thought from my anecdote about Oakhaven back to the community garden. The other plot of nature I failed to protect. "Statistically, our chances of correctly picking the Harvest Host's next target on our first try are very low. No matter how excited Fred might be."

"Then why did you invite us here, of all places?" I ask.

"Because I thought you'd like it. This is simply an evening

112

of apple picking. A normal fall activity that normal girls enjoy." She smiles at me, but it flickers out as her eyes move from my face to the lowest branches surrounding us. Most of them are picked bare already, leaving the best options on the higher branches.

"Are you afraid you aren't going to be tall enough to reach the apples?" I tease.

She swats at me. "Oh, shut up!"

I giggle as she chases me down the row of trees. *Since when do I giggle?* "You already said I'm an expert!" I yell. "You shouldn't bully your only chance of coming back with apples that aren't scavenged from the ground and full of worms."

I stop at a tree deep enough in the orchard that it's less picked over by visitors. Velma rolls her eyes at me when she approaches, but repeats my technique to pick an apple by herself. "Thank you," she says.

"I guess I'm a good tutor," I say. "It's an honor to get to teach something new to the smartest girl in Coolsville."

"Like that's doing us a ton of good right now," she chides. "I'm sorry we don't have any hard evidence to exonerate you yet. We are trying, I swear. I have an idea for an experiment—"

I stop her the same way she interrupted me before, by touching her bare arm, which she has been gesturing wildly during her nervous explanation.

"Velma, I trust you," I tell her. The only relief I've had lately is knowing Velma is on the case. I know she won't give up until she has answers. "I hope the rest of the gang knows they would be nothing without you."

She blushes furiously at that. "I'm not so crucial," she says with a breathy laugh. "Let's talk about something else. Anything but monsters . . . or how short I am."

I'm grateful for the topic change, even though it's hard to avoid thinking about the host. We pick more apples in a slightly awkward silence for a while, talking only about our latest assignment for chemistry class. I repeat the successful parts of our earlier conversation in my head, analyzing them for some clue to reignite the lighthearted feelings we had before thoughts of the specter crushed the vibe.

My comment about apple-picking tutoring reminds me of Velma's excuse for finding me in the library the other day, which finally unlocks an untouched topic of conversation.

"What did you mean when you said the founders of Coolsville would hate me?"

"Oh, that?" Velma asks casually, like she's forgotten she greeted an already distraught me with such a weird opening line. "The town founders didn't like anything that upset the status quo."

"They wouldn't like that I'm goth?" I guess.

She shakes her head. "*Serenity is the only solution for Coolsville,*" she quotes. "It's not how you look. It's your arrival in the first place. You probably noticed gossip about you was growing even before the Harvest Host showed up. Rumors are more insidious and contagious because shocking events don't happen here. There are no mysteries in Coolsville.

The current town leaders follow the Coolidges' lead. There have been no changes to the way the town operates in my whole life. When we were twelve, Daphne tried to hold a bake sale to raise money for a women's self-defense class, but the sheriff shut it down because 'only the PTA holds bake sales.'"

Velma spots another untouched tree a few yards away and hurries to pad her numbers in the unspoken competition that has developed between us.

Coolsville's commitment to being boring should be a relief to me, but it doesn't ease my mind like I thought it would. Some part of me hoped the Mystery Inc. crew were just mystery magnets and the Harvest Host just another run-of-the-mill oddity in the sea of weirdness that surrounded them. The only other time I've dealt with something this awful was during their sole visit to my hometown, so it wasn't an impossible theory. Just a mean one.

But since our move alone was enough to make news in Coolsville, it's clear I was wrong. The gang isn't surrounded by the unexplainable. Quite the opposite. The Mystery Machine, a hand-painted warning sign, is more than a garish display of color. The gang's van, their communal drive to ask questions and push boundaries—it's an open act of rebellion against Coolsville's sacred serenity.

If they had to road-trip all the way to Massachusetts to find something spooky to solve, my connection to the host can't be random.

I need to shake myself out of this before my thoughts

spark a panic attack. I close my eyes and take a deep breath, but the scent that invades my nostrils is so rancid I almost gag. I open my eyes and search for the source of the sickly sweet smell. The fading sunlight, so enchanting a moment ago, is foreboding now. The trees nearest me look fine, but then I look down and that's when I see it.

The basket of apples in my hands suddenly feels like a lead weight, and the fruits that were perfectly ripe just moments ago have begun to brown, as if aging weeks in just seconds.

"Velma?" I call, but she's still distracted by the abundant tree before her.

Then, rising from the grass, I see the lightest tendrils of glowing mist begin to form.

I drop the basket and run to Velma. I grab her hand and head back toward the orchard entrance. She doesn't even have time to ask why before we hear it.

Menacing laughter comes from all directions as the mist continues to rise from the shaded ground. Screams echo in the dark as voices I don't recognize call out names, trying to find their loved ones in the growing haze. I catch glimpses of our friends running through the increasingly foggy rows ahead of us. Fred, Luna, and Daphne run in the opposite direction from me and Velma, deeper into the orchard, with their arms full of Fred's latest contraption. I call out to them, but the mist is so bad that we can't reach them before they disappear again.

So we follow Shaggy and Scooby instead as they race

toward the distant light of the parking lot, with a crowd at their heels. Dusk's green highlights, nearly the same color as the mist, are barely visible on their tail.

Velma squeezes my hand.

"Don't worry." I cling tighter to her. "I won't let you go," I promise. I have a feeling I need to hear that more than she does.

When we exit the orchard, I trip on a root concealed by the mist. As I fall, I feel Velma pull at my arm, and I twist back to her. But my momentum is too strong, and a second later I hit the ground hard on my back. Velma falls with me and lands more softly. On top of me. We both cough to clear the mist from our lungs, but it's her that takes my breath away. Her face is just inches above mine. Her brunette bob curtains her face, her freckles a constellation pointing right to her lips. Her lips are moving. Saying something.

"My glasses!" she exclaims, rolling off me. "I've lost them!"

I worry that she lost them among the trees, but we find them near where we fell. It's for the best, because the mist has completely engulfed the orchard by now. Velma shoves her glasses back onto her face and we crawl away from the entrance.

Leaves spin like confetti in the air as they fall from previously healthy trees. The thumps of rotted apples hitting the ground are an ominous drumroll announcing the Harvest Host's presence above the decaying treetops.

"My darling witch," it taunts as more and more apple

pickers stumble out of the rotting orchard. "Where are your little friends?" it asks me. "Have they abandoned you, like you abandoned Oakhaven? Like you've abandoned who you are?" It spreads its soulless smile as it rises, growing unfathomably large above the treetops. "My prickly Thorn," it says, "I've done this all for you!"

It laughs again, and swoops low over the fleeing families. They cower where they stand, parents trying to cocoon their kids against the green mist as its features fade into the thickening fog. That's all that remains of the host yet again.

It's undeniable now. The Harvest Host has claimed me and damned me to the consequences of its actions. This is so much worse than the student garden. There were dozens of people in the orchard when the specter arrived.

People continue to crawl out of the trees like Velma and I did, but unlike us, they have a deathly pallor. Like zombies, they stumble and claw at the earth, their breath coming in harsh rasps. I can't help myself from clutching Velma's arm in terror.

"It's okay," she reassures me, but she seems shocked as well. "They're here to help. I mean, they just need help."

I let go, nodding. The prolonged exposure has left many of the innocent apple pickers coughing, choking on air they can't seem to take in. Velma waves down a familiar face in the crowd. Daphne jogs over to us.

"I'm so glad you got out," she says. "We were worried."

"Is everyone okay?" I ask.

"Our group will be fine. We got spun around in the

shadow and ended up back out here not much later than you did. Fred's all torn up," she says with a sympathetic glance back at where he's helping other victims. "We thought we'd have more time to set up his catapult, given we weren't sure if it was going to hit here. We'll be better prepared next time. But there were a lot of families here today."

"Someone has to call the police," I say. "And an ambulance."

"You're right, Thorn," Daphne says, but she doesn't look at me when she speaks. She looks at Velma instead. "Fred's calling his dad right now. They'll be here soon."

"You need to go home," Velma tells me.

"No!" I refuse. "People are hurt. I should stay and help."

"Fred will explain what happened to his father's coworkers. But you shouldn't be here when he does," Velma insists. "None of the Hex Girls should be here." Daphne nods at this like Velma's statement contains an order and takes off, I'm guessing to find the others. "It's going to look suspicious if the police find you at two crime scenes."

"It named me, Velma," I say. "I can't escape suspicion now."

She takes my hand. "I know," she says, squeezing it. "That's why you have to go."

Shaggy returns in Daphne's place, Dusk and Luna at his heels. He holds the van keys above his head like a prize. "I don't normally drive, but I've only crashed, like, two go-karts at the fair," he says. "I'll get you guys home safe."

The girls follow him and Scooby into the Mystery

Machine, leaving me no choice but to follow them. Luna closes the door behind me. Shaggy lurches the van into drive and peels out the way we came.

I watch through the rear window as Velma turns away to tend to the victims of my monster. Just once, I'd love to have a conversation with the girl I like without it being overshadowed by this awful mist.

CHAPTER FIFTEEN

My house is the farthest away, so the sun has long set by the time Shaggy drops me off. I let Scooby lick my cheek goodbye as I try to close the van door as quietly as possible. I test the doorknob to check if I need to look for the hide-a-key, but the door opens with a single turn, both a blessing and a bad omen of the odds that Dad is waiting up for me.

I try to sneak past the dining room archway to reach the stairs unspotted, but I don't make it. "Sally," my dad says, silhouetted in the dark like an anonymous source in a documentary. My name comes out as more of a relieved exhale than an actual word. "Where have you been?"

"Out," I say. I keep walking toward the stairs. Lying in wait for me doesn't work if I don't follow his guilt trip to the dinner table.

"Where are you going?" he calls.

I don't respond. He repeats himself, but I'm halfway up the stairs and I keep ignoring him. I don't stop until I reach the top, when he whips out the big guns.

"Sally McKnight!" he yells, full-naming me with the might of an army commander. I spin around on the landing, listening but not apologizing. "Where were you?" he asks again.

"At the apple orchard with the band and the gang," I confess in a monotone. He's quiet, waiting for me to elaborate, but that's all he's getting out of me. I'm not ready to talk about what happened. More than that, my dad is the last person who has a right to lecture me about keeping secrets.

He knows that, which is why he doesn't press further when I say I'm tired and going to bed. Even with my bedroom door closed, I hear him follow me up the stairs. The shadow of his feet lingers outside my door in the dim hall light for a few minutes, but he doesn't knock and I don't invite him in.

I watch the door even after he walks away, though I don't know why. He doesn't open it in my dreams either.

I thought I was ready for round two when I come downstairs the following morning, but I'm not prepared for Dad having backup.

Literal backup.

Two police officers are sitting where my father wanted me to last night, one of them nursing coffee from *my* mug. Neither of them is Sheriff Jones, but I can tell by the additional lines on Dad's face that they've found out what the Harvest Host said before it disappeared last night. I bet they aren't chalking it up to coincidence.

"Good morning, Ms. McKnight," the one drinking from my mug greets me. He's unfamiliar, but his partner is the rookie from the community garden. He looks just as eager to impress his superior as he was the first time. He gestures at the only seat left as if I'm the guest in *his* home. I hate that I have no choice but to take it.

"There was another incident last night," the young officer says.

"With that thing from the garden at your school," Dad says. "At the orchard," he adds, like this is brand-new information to me. "I told them you were there with some friends earlier in the afternoon, but you were back here by dinnertime."

"I was?" I realize only after I speak that he's trying to give me an alibi. I work hard to keep my face from betraying how surprising his loyalty to me is. "I was," I repeat, more firmly. "We had spaghetti."

"We're new to town," Dad says. "I don't like Thorn staying out late when we're still so unfamiliar with the area. She knows how seriously I take curfew."

"I do."

"If only we could take you seriously, Mr. McKnight," the mug-stealer says. "We are well aware of how new you both are to our fine town. And we also know why you came." He holds out an open hand to the rookie, who fills it with a file folder. He flips the folder open as he puts it on our dining table.

MCKNIGHT, TOWN PHARMACIST, ONE OF MANY IMPLICATED IN 'WITCH'S GHOST' SCAM IN OAKHAVEN, MASSACHUSETTS, reads the headline of an article stapled to the folder.

"About that," Dad says, "it wasn't criminal. It was only meant to help increase tourism. The mayor was involved, too! And there turned out to actually be a witch—"

The rude cop raises a hand to stop him. "Maybe people are more quaint and superstitious on the East Coast, but don't let the hippie stereotypes of Californians fool you. The Coolsville Police Department will not fall for tales about monsters over legitimate evidence."

"We'd like to ask you about what you saw last night," the rookie says to me.

"I told you," Dad says. "She wasn't there."

"There's only one witch I wish to discuss today. The

one your daughter claims to be," the older cop says. "Your band sings songs about enchanting people, and these very articles"—he taps the printouts in the folder—"say you claimed to 'do' magic in the very scam your father was implicated in."

"I wasn't involved in what he did," I spit out before I can stop myself. Dad's face falls. "I mean," I try to course-correct, "he's right that what he did wasn't criminal." It was only run-of-the-mill lying and betrayal. "I didn't have anything to do with the stuff in Oakhaven. I practiced Wicca before we moved, but *not* since then."

"Wicca, witchcraft. One and the same scammery to me," Officer Pain-in-the-Ass says. "Your wife was one of those too, am I correct?" he asks Dad. "We're told she dealt in snake oil cures before you two got married."

"That's enough," Dad says. He rises from his chair and comes to stand behind me. The condescending cop pauses in his defamation of my dead mother. Dad grips the back of my chair with both hands and speaks with the same authority as when he used my full name last night. "You are no longer welcome in my home or to speak to my underage daughter without the presence of our lawyer."

He walks the cops to the door and slams it behind them.

I don't wait for him to return to the living room. I'm already at the top of the stairs before he realizes I left, and I don't turn back when he calls me. I lock my bedroom door and slide to the floor against it. The small rush of solidarity from my father's support has evaporated with the reminder of his involvement in that stupid scam. I knew his betrayal back home would haunt us no matter where we moved, but no one was ever supposed to accuse my mother of being a criminal, too.

I know my mother never defrauded anyone, but no one in Coolsville should know anything about her at all. She practiced Wicca before I was born, and because she died so long ago it wasn't common knowledge in town. Only Mystery Inc. and the Hex Girls knew that my mom's history was the reason I was tasked with sealing Sarah Ravencroft back into her cursed spell book. It was not in any records. Never published anywhere.

I yank my phone off the charger and send a quick message in our band group chat, then hit the video call button at the top of the screen.

Thorn: Emergency meeting, answer immediately.

"Tell me you didn't," I say when Dusk's face pops up on-screen, her hair still in her sleep bonnet. Luna appears around the third time I repeat my plea.

"I don't even know what you're talking about," Dusk says, yawning. "You're the one who called the meeting. Why don't you tell us what the issue is?"

"Dusk is right, Thorn," Luna says, "though she could have phrased it nicer. What's wrong? Tell us so we can help you."

"That's the problem." My voice breaks. "What's wrong is that I can't trust one of you, and I'm pretty sure I know who."

"What's that supposed to mean?" Dusk asks, suddenly more awake. But she's no longer looking at me through her phone camera. She's looking at something off-screen, or maybe at Luna's chat bubble.

"The cops were at my house this morning," I tell them. "They came to ask about last night, but they knew about my mom. They accused her of selling snake oil cures. They knew she was Wiccan. That shouldn't be possible."

"You're right," Luna says, confused. "They shouldn't have known that."

Dusk doesn't say anything. I didn't expect her to, because all of her behavior lately suddenly makes sense. Her standoffishness. Her suspiciously subdued temper when we were being mocked at school. The way she's intentionally walled herself off not only from our new friends but from the band too.

"I didn't mean for Jordan to use it against you!" Dusk finally confesses.

"Oh, okay, that makes it all fine," I snap. "You didn't know that the girl whose first words to me were insults would use my real name and my mother's history against me. My bad. I'm sorry. I have nothing to be pissed off about!"

"She's not like that with everyone else," Dusk argues. "She was—she *is* nice to me in the class we have together. She listened about how much it sucked not to share classes with either of you. She's learning how to play drums and appreciated my advice. I'm sorry. I didn't have anyone else."

I can't muster forgiveness to my lips, or to even accept

her apology. "You had me" is all I can think to say, but it's not enough.

"No, I didn't!" she pushes back. "I didn't have anyone and you had everyone! You always have everyone! We came here because *you* already had friends here. We came here for you so the band didn't have to split up. We did this all for you and you don't even care!"

"Dusk—" Luna starts.

"No, Luna, you know exactly what I'm talking about. I'm tired of repeatedly ruining my life for someone who only cares about herself. You can keep making nice all you want, but I tried. I tried! I'm done." She rage-quits the call to get the last word, leaving Luna and me alone.

"I care about you both." I don't know what else to say.

"I know you do," Luna says, "so please don't take this the wrong way, but I have to go be with her." She raises her voice as I open my mouth to respond. "I'm not taking sides! I'm not. But you have all your new friends, Thorn. She just has me. I'll try to talk her down, but . . ." The screen buffers in the silence of her unfinished sentence. We both know this won't repair itself overnight. "I'm still here for you," she says. "I love you."

"But you have to stick with her."

"I have to. I'm sorry."

"Don't be. I'll be fine," I tell her.

It's only after she hangs up that I wonder if that's a lie.

CHAPTER SIXTEEN

I watch Coolsville fade from the rear window with an empty sort of déjà vu. As we drive, I can't decide whether I wish this was permanent or I'm simply grateful for a short distraction. The gang didn't have to invite me along on this supply-sourcing expedition, but I'm excited to visit a new town. To go somewhere where no one knows or resents me.

Crystal Cove isn't what I expected, though.

Even the welcome sign is weathered; no polished beach billboards here. Fred slows the Mystery Machine as we drive into town, careful to avoid potholes. He pulls over on a main street of sorts. The shops look untouched by the last few decades of design and basic maintenance, like we're on the set of movie shot in the nineties. It's the exact opposite of Coolsville's bright colors and *serenity*.

"We'll be back in an hour or so," Fred says as Velma and I slip out the back of the van. She nods while I stand there awkwardly like a kid at a family reunion, surrounded by people and places everyone else knows better than me.

I know the plan: Velma and I are to visit the occult bookstore to look into magical solutions to the host, while the others shop for supplies for Fred's next trap.

That doesn't mean I feel any less like a fifth wheel. Or a sixth, if you count Scooby. He places his paws against the window as they drive away, barking in alarm as if Velma and I have been accidentally forgotten. I think of how amused Dusk would be by Scooby's misplaced distress. Ever since my fight with her three days ago, Mystery Inc.'s closeness hurts my broken heart. My chest feels empty instead of filled by their welcoming spirit. They are great friends, but I'll never have the same connection with them as I do—as I *did* with Dusk and Luna.

One look at the bookstore makes it clear this is the store where Velma bought the book on Wicca she gifted me. The door chimes when it closes behind us, but I can't spot where the sound came from. Multiple tarot card decks sit in the faded window, each painted a different way but equally ready to give the same dark fortunes.

I avoid them as I follow Velma through the store. My nose tickles with a sneeze at the contrasting smells of the herbal concoctions locked in the glass counter guarded by a wrinkled woman who watches us with kind eyes.

"Hello, Velma," she says warmly.

"You're a regular, huh?" I joke to make myself more at ease and resist the urge to run. Velma rolls her eyes at me so affectionately it nearly throws me off balance and I almost walk right into a bookshelf. I look away from her and scan the shelves for a distraction—because apparently I'd rather think about magic than the feeling Velma's teasing creates in my stomach. There's a wide selection of books here for a shop so niche as to focus solely on the occult. Some books are so new their dust jackets shine in the light from the dusty window. Others look even older than the shopkeeper.

"Miss Thomas, this is my friend Thorn," Velma tells the shopkeeper. "She recently moved to Coolsville from the East Coast."

"Welcome to California, Thorn," Miss Thomas says. I flounder like a fish, waving hello with a shy smile. "What brings the two of you to my shop today?"

"We're looking for books on spectral possession and land curses," Velma says. Miss Thomas points toward the far left corner of the shop. Velma sets off, then doubles back when I don't immediately follow.

She offers her hand to guide me. I take it, despite my apprehension being here.

The touch of her palm calms me as she leads me through a

maze of everything I came to California to avoid. Hauntings. Possession. Monsters. Witches. *Fate.* She browses one-handed when she reaches her destination, stealing glances at me every few minutes to make sure I'm not about to bolt.

As long as she keeps holding my hand, I won't go anywhere. I honestly don't know where I'd run to, anyway. When this trip was first pitched to me, I naively assumed we'd go to some generic shopping plaza. A chain bookstore, a hardware store, a drive-through for dinner. Crystal Cove is . . . not that.

"Why are we here, again?" I ask Velma.

She's smart enough to understand I'm not talking about the bookstore. "We come to Crystal Cove for supplies and access to records that Coolsville doesn't have." She tips a book from the shelf to inspect its cover. "Or ones they refuse to give us," she amends with a sarcastic grin. "Crystal Cove tends to be the destination for anything too unsightly for Coolsville. It's probably where the gang and I will end up. Eventually."

"Is that what you want?"

She pushes the book back onto the shelf and dances her thin fingers farther down the row, consulting the titles with the list she made on her phone. I wait in the comfortable silence, feeling calmer with my hand in hers.

"No," she says, quickly and quietly. "I love my town," she admits, "but I don't think it loves people like me."

I don't have anything positive to say to that, so I squeeze her hand like she did mine in the orchard. *I understand how you're feeling,* my squeeze says. *I'm here. I won't let you go.*

She gently releases her hold on me to pull the book she's looking at from the shelf, along with another that catches her interest on our way back to the front of the store. After she places her haul on the counter, she offers me her hand again. I'm so pleased I gain the courage to poke about while the shopkeeper tallies up the sale.

At the counter, a book is on display. I pick it up with my free hand. *Crystal & Gold: The Story of Two Towns and Manifest Destiny,* the title page reads. The cover features two old photos of early Coolsville and Crystal Cove that are divided by a zigzagging gold line. Velma leans over to take a look. I can smell her floral shampoo from where her bob hovers beneath my chin. I want to ask her what the scent is, but that would be a very off-topic jump from our current focus.

Could it be rose? No. Maybe it's a mixture with some sort of spice . . .

"It's not really an occult book," Miss Thomas admits, noticing what has drawn our attention. "We're carrying it because it's a new book on our history written by a local author."

Velma adds it to her pile.

"I hope that's for you," I say. "You've already bought me a book."

She laughs. "It's so cute that you think I would stop at one," she says.

My brain short-circuits at her calling me cute—well, she

didn't technically say that *I* was cute. She finds my doubt in her commitment to improving my knowledge "cute." Still, it feels like it counts.

I'm lost in this merry-go-round of gay panic when Fred bursts through the door I don't think his sudden arrival would be enough to stop my mental spiraling if Velma didn't also drop my hand at the exact same time. She lets go so quickly I almost tip over as I instinctively reach for her hand, but she's already moved it to the counter, counting out her change.

Well, that's weird . . . Miss Thomas didn't demand we hurry up the transaction. There's no explanation for why Velma let go of me so quickly unless she didn't want Fred to see us. But why would she be worried about that? There's nothing wrong with friends holding hands . . . unless she didn't mean the gesture in a purely platonic manner?

"I can't believe he did this!" Fred yells.

Ms. Thomas is unfazed by his dramatic entrance. It seems like this isn't the first time Mystery Inc. has held an impromptu team meeting in her shop.

I've never seen Fred so incensed. I don't know if I've ever seen him mad, but he's *furious* now. He paces the aisles of the small bookshop, fuming. Daphne comes in through the chiming door, less angry but equally hurried, with Scooby and Shaggy right behind her. I back up a bit to make space.

"We'll find another way, Freddie," Daphne says. She goes after their unraveling leader as he disappears down another aisle. Velma raises an eyebrow at Shaggy.

"The shops won't sell to us anymore," he says.

"None of them!" Fred laments from deep within the stacks.

"They said the sheriff of Coolsville commanded they stop supplying his son with 'tools of vandalism and destruction.'" Shaggy makes air quotes around this last part, stabbing the air with his fingers hooked sharp like vampire fangs. "Even the diner refused to take our order," he adds.

Scooby whines at this statement, panting like he hasn't eaten in days even though I gave him three treats on the drive here.

I turn back to Velma and our unfinished order resting on the counter.

Miss Thomas doesn't bother looking up from the register as she finishes the sale. "No one bans me from selling books," she says. "Have a nice day."

CHAPTER SEVENTEEN

I know my life is broken, because even music isn't enough to soothe my soul anymore. The rumblings of the acts ahead of our slot in the talent show rehearsal shouldn't stress me. If I know one thing, it's that our band is great. My place in this show is the most normal part of my life right now.

I watch a magician make his partner's backpack disappear to light applause from the teachers assigned to supervise the rehearsal. "If only 'my homework was erased from this mortal plane of existence' was a valid excuse," the young magician jokes. Luna giggles at this, adding another piece of evidence to my long-term conspiracy board of her using goth aesthetics as a cover for her true passion: being a total dork.

I let go of the curtain. "I'm gonna go check on Dusk," I say.

Luna side-eyes me from her perch, but doesn't move to follow me. "Good luck."

Find common ground, I remind myself, like I'm gearing up for a conversation with a stranger instead of my best friend. I've been trying my best to understand Dusk's choices. I know she had every reason to feel lonely and isolated. I want to forgive her.

But then I walk in on something like this, and every thought of fairness inside me sparks out. Jordan is leaning against the ivory-painted back wall, looking over sheet music with Dusk. "I was thinking of changing it here." She points at the paper.

Dusk shakes her head, a noise of lighthearted disgust escaping her lips. "If you hold the note, it will have more impact," she says.

Jordan pulls out a pen tucked behind her ear and braces the page against her knee to annotate. "If you say so," she says, writing. "I'm up next. See you later." She's so distracted, she doesn't see me as she walks backward right into my chest. "Watch where you're going," she snaps before continuing to the stage.

I raise my arms in exasperation as I close the distance

to Dusk. "You see that?" I ask rhetorically. "She walked into me, not the other way around. She needs to take her own advice."

"You could have warned her," Dusk says. "You saw her coming your way."

"So did you," I bite out. There's so much I want to talk to her about, but I can't risk a fight minutes before a performance. *You didn't share our practice sheets with her, did you? You have to know she's playing you. Do you know why she has it in for me?* The irony of the fury I'd unleash by accusing Dusk of being too kind for her own good is not lost on me.

There's no need to question Dusk's motives, because I know she wouldn't harm the band intentionally. But she won't admit that she harmed us anyway. She hurt me by giving Jordan information about my past, and seeing her continue to pal around with Jordan digs the knife in deeper each time. That girl *hates* me.

Dusk is like my sister. She's supposed to love me.

Now I can't talk to her. She and Luna are usually the first people I tell about anything that happens in my life. I want to talk to Dusk about how different California is from Massachusetts. I want to ask her how her little siblings are adjusting to the move. I want her to talk me out of spiraling, because I can't stop replaying Velma dropping my hand in the bookshop over and over again. I'm starting to wonder if Velma could have feelings for me too. I need to dissect all the hand holding and too-long eye contact that has me more puzzled than the actual mystery we're investigating. I need advice and guidance from my best friend.

I even want to discuss the Harvest Host, especially with Mystery Inc. so on edge after being banned from nearly every shop in Crystal Cove. Increasingly outlandish ideas have been lobbed back and forth in the shared group chat as they try to figure out how to prepare for the next attack, which feels inevitable at this point.

I know Dusk has seen the chat. She and Luna are both still in it, though neither of them responds anymore. It's just me among a different group of lifelong friends.

I'm overthinking everything.

"We're up next!" Luna calls out halfway between us and the curtain, pausing only long enough to confirm we're coming before returning to the spot where she's watched the other acts perform all afternoon.

"The Hex Girls," the drama teacher reads from the call list. "I'm going to read off names to confirm you are the same act from auditions. Please respond like roll call as I say your name. Jane Brooks?"

"Here," Dusk says. She wiggles around on the seat at the drum set, finding the best spot.

"Kimberly Hale?"

"Ready!" Luna chirps from the keyboard. She's smiling so wide all her teeth show, unbearably excited to perform. I'm so jealous of her joy I don't hear my name the first time it's called.

"Thorn McKnight?"

"Sorry, I'm here," I say.

"Maybe you should've called for Sally instead," someone jeers. I glare at Jordan, but she doesn't move from stage left as the music starts and my cue creeps up and almost misses me. I tear my gaze from her and try to focus on the empty seats that will be packed the next time I'm up here. I attempt to wipe my mind of distractions real and imagined, but I can't shake the unease that's rattled my internal beat counter.

I miss another cue and twist my head to apologize to the girls, but as I do the lights flicker. Looking up, I see one of the stage lights break away from its metal casing and careen right toward me. Before I can even think about ducking, someone yanks me back, and the light whizzes past me to crash on the edge of the stage, then bounces off it, toward the judges.

The teachers scream as they scurry away from the light, but I can barely hear them. My heartbeat fills up my eardrums from the adrenaline. I should have been crushed beneath the light or tossed from the stage, but instead I was pulled back. Out of the line of fire. By Dusk. She leaped from the drums to save me, sacrificing one of her lucky drumsticks to do it.

I roll off the cracked drumstick. "I'm sorry," I say. "And thank you."

Dusk waves me off. "Don't make a big deal about it," she says, sweeping the drumstick remnants toward herself without looking at me. "Can't win without a vocalist."

"Are you okay?" the drama teacher asks us, suddenly a lot more passionate about our act than she was a few minutes ago. I look at Luna, who thankfully is fine, though shell-shocked. She nods, hands still frozen above the keyboard.

"Thank goodness," the drama teacher says. "Okay, off the stage. Rehearsal is canceled. We'll email a notice with a rescheduled date once we can assure your safety." She shepherds us off the stage, stopping shy of apologizing, probably to protect the school from a lawsuit. "I promise we will do a thorough inspection for damage. Nothing like this will happen again."

I think she's right. I don't think this will happen again, at least not in the exact same way. When I look up at where the light hung, I can't see an obvious fault. A smudge of gold that could be rust might have been the cause of the break. But still, I don't think they'll find any natural damage.

Not if the smirk on Jordan's face is anything to go by.

CHAPTER EIGHTEEN

When Velma told me about the plan, she opened with all the benefits the successful completion of it would bring to the investigation. "I'm telling you this first because you probably won't like what we're planning to do," she said.

She was right.

I try to focus on the positives: The gang is finally wearing darker clothing. Fred is hopeful again, a state of being so ingrained in his personality that I hadn't realized how empty he would seem without it until it disappeared. And finally, it's *technically* not breaking in when you have a key.

Daphne unlocks the building with the key she was given by her journalism teacher to allow her early access to the student broadcast studio for morning announcements. She reminds us to put the flashlights on our phones on the lowest setting, because the night janitor sometimes doubles back on his rounds. I try not to think about how many times the gang must have done this to know that.

"All right, gang, let's split up," Fred says. "Daph, you'll stay here as lookout. Shaggy, you and Scoob come with me to the woodshop for supplies. And, Velms and Thorn, you've got an experiment to do in the chem lab."

Again I try *very* hard not to think about how many times they've done this.

The halls are cavernous when empty. Doubly so in the dark, where the shadows melt the edges and expand the length into an endless abyss. I follow Velma's too-sure steps, guided by the glow of my flashlight kissing her calves. When I'm not watching her feet, I'm looking over my shoulder, still majorly spooked after the lighting incident at rehearsal the other day.

I hold the door of the chemistry classroom open for Velma, but that's where my usefulness ends. She doesn't need me for the next part. I'm more of a liability than an asset on this mission. I'm only necessary for the second part of the plan, but I don't want to think about that.

That's tomorrow's problem, if all goes well tonight.

I watch in admiration as Velma gathers beakers and

solutions for her experiment. She gestures for me to come closer, and when I do, she places a hand on my waist while she digs with her other hand into the bag she had me carry. She pulls out several samples of soil, one of which I'm sure contains the dirt she took from the community garden the afternoon of the original attack.

She has four different samples total, despite the fact the Harvest Host has only struck twice so far. "Control samples," she answers my unspoken question.

I nod like that explains everything. I don't know why she chose to let me replace her lab partner in class, because I clearly am of no help when it comes to scientific experiments of any kind. She's going to be the only reason I pass chemistry, if I don't mar her perfect record instead.

"Do you think the new plan will work?" I ask.

"I think," Velma says slowly, her words as drawn out as the liquid she's carefully adding to her quartet of mud, "that we will stop the specter soon. I have a hypothesis and Fred's plan is possible, if a little unorthodox."

It's not a definitive answer either way, but I don't push her for fear of causing an explosion, or whatever else might happen if her experiment goes wrong. She won't tell me what she's doing or what her hypothesis might be, and while I know Velma is basically a genius, the secrecy starts to drain my confidence in tomorrow's plan like the excess sediment she's rinsing away.

"Velma?" I ask. She looks up at me from her mini mad-science lab, her eyes glittering thanks to the combination of the beaker's reflection and her love of the scientific process. "You're a rational, logical person," I say.

She laughs and then tries to smother it at the serious look on my face. I don't mind. I like the sound, even when I'm as anxious as I am right now. "Yes?" She controls herself enough to prompt me to continue.

"Well," I start, my palms sweaty against the cold table. "Your friends aren't always as convinced there's a reasonable explanation for your mysteries. You came to Oakhaven because Ben Ravencroft asked you to debunk the witch's ghost—"

"Actually, he didn't," Velma says. "He didn't tell us about his ancestor's reputation until we were already in Oakhaven. He lied about a lot of things."

"He definitely did," I agree. "But still, *you* did try to debunk it, even when Shaggy and Scooby thought the Hex Girls and I were evil witches. Obviously they were wrong, but they were right about something paranormal going on. Dogs are historically very attuned to that, you know."

"Do you want me to tell you the answer to the Harvest Host won't be paranormal?" Velma asks, seeing where I'm going with my rambling.

I look out the window, grateful the ruined garden is not close enough to be visible in the dark. "I like the idea of life without ghosts and monsters, even if I know better," I say. "I just wanted Coolsville to be different . . . safer."

"Ignoring what's uncomfortable is not the same thing as staying safe," Velma says. She's quiet for a long moment.

"But for what it's worth, I'm hopeful we'll find the answers to the host in these experiments."

Her face glows above the bright colors boiling on the Bunsen burner. She looks like a witch brewing potions. I start to tell her as much, but the thought reminds me of what the gang asked me to do tomorrow and my joke dies on my lips.

"If you believe in science so much, why even consider a magical answer?" I ask.

"Sir Arthur Conan Doyle once wrote 'When you have eliminated the impossible, whatever remains, however improbable, must be the truth.' We are eliminating the impossible," Velma says. She twists the dial on the burner, reducing the heat. "Science itself looks like magic if you don't understand it."

I'm not sure I understand anything right now, and while I'm sure Velma wasn't trying to make me feel worse, her easy acceptance that this could be magic has me spiraling. "I'm gonna go check the hall to make sure it's clear," I say, needing a moment to myself.

Velma nods, too wrapped up in her experiment to notice my distress. "I should be done with the burner in a few minutes and then the samples should be stable enough to stash. It will probably take a few days for results."

"Sounds good." I let myself out into the hall to silence the other questions on my tongue. They aren't related to the experiment, and the more I ponder them, the less sure I am I want answers. Talking with Velma—more like begging her to assure me that the Harvest Host won't turn out to be supernatural—has opened a Pandora's box inside me, poisoning my already paranoid mind with thoughts I can't afford to dwell on.

The hall is unchanged, so I edge down it to take in details I don't have time for during the day. In a trophy case on the wall two classrooms down, a photo of the original Coolsville schoolhouse is displayed. It was a small building, probably no bigger than two or three rooms. I remember a similar photo back home, though Oakhaven's schoolhouse never expanded much beyond that. It doubled, if you could claim that much. Nothing like this campus.

My life here was supposed to be different. This should have been a fresh start, but it's just brought new complications. Everything feels so wrong. The anxiety. The fear. The confusion. The cold.

Wait.

When did it get so cold?

The hall lights are off, but the trophy case has its own light, to illuminate the medals and faded yearbook photos. I back away from the display, suppressing a shiver, as the glow begins to fade and then flash, like it also needs to shake off the cold.

I try to focus on the dimmer spots, away from the trophy case, looking for an air-conditioning sensor I could have motion activated. I don't see anything. The trophy case flickers again, as do the three other display cases farther down the hall.

In the distance, I see a flickering shadow. It moves with each flash of light, getting closer. I tuck myself behind the jut of the nearest case, hoping it's not the janitor.

"You don't belong here," a voice calls out. It sounds angry and ancient and scratches at my skull. "You're ruining this town."

That doesn't sound like an underpaid janitor.

I hurriedly pull out the paper with the banishing chant I'm supposed to be practicing for tomorrow. My voice is shaky as I attempt to recite the spell Velma helped me pick out of the Wiccan book she gave me. "Spirit, you don't belong here," I say. The lights flicker again. I close my eyes and inhale deeply. "This is not the place for you. Your time has come. You must *go*."

When I open my eyes, the hall is as it was. The figure still looms in the distance, facing me. Through the light of the display, I can make out an ascot tail jutting from its neck and I breathe a deep sigh of relief. "Fred?" I ask, confused.

The figure doesn't respond.

A clatter behind me makes me spin around, but I don't see anything. I start to turn back around when a hand grips my shoulder.

I nearly scream, but it really is Fred after all.

"What's happening with the lights over here?" he asks me.

I double over, gripping my head with both hands as I stumble away from him and try to catch my breath. "I don't know," I admit.

Fred gently helps me back to a standing position. "Are you

okay?" he asks. I step out of his concerned hold, shrugging in what I hope looks like a casual way.

"Yeah, yeah," I say. "I'm fine." I squint into the darkness. "I just . . . don't know what that was."

"Whatever it was, we should go," Fred says. "It'll probably draw the janitor this way soon. I'll get the others, you get Velma."

I slip back into the chemistry classroom, never more grateful to get off campus. And that's really saying something.

CHAPTER NINETEEN

The next evening, Scooby yawns lazily where he rests below the large gourd I'm sitting on in the pumpkin patch. "Aren't you supposed to be protecting me?" I joke. He props himself up at attention and gives me a big lick on the face. "Okay, okay," I laugh, pushing him back down. "I'm sorry for doubting you."

Scooby doesn't lie down again. Instead he swivels his big head around to survey the growing crowd of young families and couples. Then he whines a little, nuzzling his head against my hand. "I'm scared too," I admit.

I want to tell him that the Harvest Host might not even show, but Velma and Fred seem much more confident of the odds than they did at the orchard. Velma tried to explain her reasoning for this stakeout on the drive here, but my mind went blank after she mentioned how packed the pumpkin patch would likely be. She wasn't wrong. This place is crawling, in some cases literally, with children and parents.

I don't want the host to ruin such a nice day for all these innocent families, but I also don't know what I'll do if this doesn't work. I need this destruction to end. Luna has kept me updated on Dusk, who seems to be doing just fine without me, but I'm worried that if this goes on for much longer it will fracture the band forever. We have never gone this long without a band practice. I like the gang, but the Hex Girls are my soul sisters. I can't lose them.

Shaggy heads toward us with an armful of pumpkins. "Are those part of the trap?" I ask, even though I suspect I already know the answer.

He shakes his head. "Nope," he says, popping the *p*. "I figured we could banish two ghosts with one very tasty stone. Scoob, wanna pick out one for yourself?"

Scooby looks to me for approval. He remembers his watchdog task and doesn't want to get in trouble. "It's okay," I tell him, scratching him behind one ear. "You've been a very good boy. Go pick out a treat." He trots over happily and sniffs the options nearby, then picks up a small pumpkin between his teeth and follows Shaggy to the Mystery Machine to stash what they found.

It's better that I'm alone if the specter shows up. I'm tired of people getting hurt, and I'm tired of the real culprit—whoever or whatever it is—dragging my name through the rotted remains of the crops they kill.

The plan is a two-pronged approach. I'm supposed to stay where I am as strategically placed bait while Fred, Daphne, and Velma staff a makeshift face-painting booth with a large canopy that has a quick-release spring to ensnare the specter. If the Harvest Host is a physical being, this should capture it.

If it's not a physical being, if it's something different, something more . . . In that case, I'm solely responsible for the execution of plan B. I finger the banishing spell in my pocket and hope I don't need to use it. It wasn't effective last night, and the weirdness with the lights doesn't bode well for the chance of the host not being supernatural.

There's a normal explanation for this, I tell myself. It will all be over soon.

Seemingly timed to mock me, the telltale mist begins to form across the pumpkin patch. It's much more noticeable in the early-afternoon light than it was in the twilight of the orchard.

I spot the rest of the gang watching me from the face-painting booth as Scooby and Shaggy return from storing their pumpkin haul. Shaggy hooks a finger in Scooby's teal collar, scratching the fur on his neck at a pace that doesn't look calming for either of them. "I don't see the host," he says.

Neither do I, but the mist is still forming.

An unspoken question rises with the mist around us: Do we wait it out? We're prepared to confront the specter, but there are so many people here. There are children here. The victims of the orchard attack recovered quickly with medical help, but a few kids and older people had coughs that lasted for days afterward. No one else should get sick in our quest to capture the host. I can't be responsible for that.

The right choice is obvious. I race to the nearest bystander, urging them to leave. When I turn around to look for someone else to warn, I see Shaggy and Scooby running in a different direction to help a family maneuver their stroller through the bumpy escape route. The remaining members of Mystery Inc. abandon the carefully constructed trap to do the same.

We've almost cleared the area when a horribly familiar presence makes itself known.

"Leaving so soon?" the Harvest Host asks, hovering above once-healthy pumpkins.

In an open area like this, its visage is more overwhelming than before. We heard more than saw it in the orchard, and the school garden had too many distractions. Here, with nowhere to run and the entire sky to poison, the mist feels claustrophobic and heavy, like arms reaching to drag me underground.

I want to flee with the bystanders, but I hold my ground. The host creeps toward me as the gang sprints to their station. They can still spring the trap, but only if I lead the host to the right place.

"Why won't you leave me alone?" I shout. I try to make my backtracking look panicked and unplanned instead of what it really is: a deliberate trail to the gang's trap. My frazzled and frustrated tone isn't fake, though.

"I'm here for you," it says, the words like cracks of thunder after a lightning burst. "Because of you."

I keep walking backward. "Why?" I shout. "Why do all this destruction in my name? I'm not even from Coolsville."

"That's the point, dearest Thorn!" Its storm-colored mouth opens wider than my head as the morphing body glides after me. "You don't belong here. You should go back home. Repent for what you did to the Ravencrofts. Leave Coolsville."

"I can't go back," I say as I fall into the large pumpkin I was originally sitting on, now a putrid, decaying shell.

The host closes in on me just as Fred yells, "Now!" I hear ropes snapping, and a rush of air whooshes past me. I'm almost blinded by the mist the flying tent upsets around me. The sky clears for a fraction of a second, the Harvest Host becoming slightly more transparent as it pivots to go after the gang. The tarp flies through the host and falls onto the pumpkins beneath it. The host rises higher above my friends, expanding and growing darker with every breath they cough out.

It couldn't be contained by the physical trap because it's not corporeal.

It's up to me now.

I swallow saliva to soothe my suddenly dry throat as I bring the note out of my pocket. It's hard to read in the obscuring fog, especially now that the paper is soaked in rotten pumpkin goo. "Spirit, you don't belong here," I say. "This is not the place for you. Your time has come. You must go."

The host laughs at me, unbothered.

I try again, stuttering, but it's no use. "Ah, my rogue Thorn," the host chides. "Your efforts are misguided. We are one and the same. You'll see."

The host disappears just like before, leaving us in the aftermath after thwarting two attempts to capture it in less than ten minutes.

I hear my friends calling my name as they search for me in the fog, but I'm too disappointed to answer them. "Thorn," Velma cries the loudest. "Thorn!"

Scooby finds me first. He nudges my hand until I grip his collar, then guides me through the mist, barking like a car alarm to signal our location until the others find us. Fred squeezes me tight at the edge of the parking lot.

"I'm so sorry," he says. "The plan failed. It's my fault. Are you all right?"

"I'm fine," I say, my reassurance undercut by the cough that punctuates it.

Velma makes a noise, but when I turn to look at her, Daphne rushes me into a hug instead.

"I'm really okay," I promise. "I should be the one

apologizing. I couldn't get the spell right. I let you guys down."

"We can try again," Daphne says. "Right?"

Shaggy lets out a noncommittal hum as he bends to hug Scooby. I let go of Scooby's collar so they can embrace. Fred's face is ashen, his attention locked on the fading fog, but he nods. "Totally," he says. "We'll try something else. We're not giving up."

Velma stalks off. Her shoes slap hard against the pavement as she leaves the gang behind to clean up the mess of the failed trap. That's not like her, so I follow behind. She stops under an awning off the pumpkin patch's barn.

"You could have gotten hurt," she says when I catch up to her, sounding even more upset than the others. "I'm so sorry we put you in that position."

"That was always a risk," I remind her. "We couldn't have known it wouldn't work unless we tried it. It was an experiment."

"A failed experiment," Velma says, pouting.

"Is it a failure if it confirms a theory, even if it isn't the one you hoped for?" I ask. "I think most scientists would consider that a success." I smile at her, hoping this nerdy talk will cheer her up some. She doesn't smile back.

I don't want her to blame herself. If anyone failed tonight, it was me.

Velma clenches and unclenches her fists repeatedly, tapping one knee-high-clad foot anxiously against the post she's leaning on.

"That isn't the point," she says. "I just hate that you were in danger."

"Isn't being in danger normal for you?" I ask.

Velma presses her palms against her eyes. "It's not the same," she says, her sweet voice breaking. "It's different when it's you."

I stare at her as she lowers her hands and tips her head back to trap the tears that have started forming in her eyes. I'm frozen where I stand, afraid to touch her. More terrified of the question I'm about to ask than I could be of any monster.

"What's different about me?"

Velma doesn't answer. She tilts her head back down, looking up at me through those waterlogged brown eyes. Then something changes in her expression. Her eyes go from lost to determined, like she has found the answer to a question she's been asking for a while. She rises on her tiptoes, and like a magnet, I fall, leaning forward until our lips touch.

We stumble back into the post. Her hands cradle my chin, then trail desperately to my neck, clinging to me like she'd fall to pieces otherwise. I hold tight to her, to this moment. A light in this endless haze. Something good amid the disaster. Kissing Velma feels like it could bring all the plants back to life.

A rotted branch snaps under my foot and the blissful moment ends.

Velma pushes me away and steps back. She looks around,

eyes wild as she desperately searches for the source of the noise.

Oh. Finally I've solved a mystery before my friends did.

"No one saw us," I say gently, "but would it be such a disaster if they did?" I know the Mystery Inc. crew. They would never treat Velma differently if they knew about us . . . whatever *us* means. They would be happy for her. I'm certain of it.

"You don't—" Velma begins, but she stops herself. It's too late. I know what she was going to say. *You don't understand.* But I understand better than anyone. "I stand out enough as is. We all do."

I want to argue the point further, but what ground do I have to stand on? I'm no stranger to standing out, intentionally or otherwise. Coming out wasn't a big deal for me, even as a sixth grader in a small town. When you reject the status quo so much already, people tend to make a million different assumptions. They never really bother to question what is the truth from what is just gossip.

I didn't care that people judged me for my goth wardrobe and makeup choices, so admitting I liked girls—and only girls—wasn't that much of an upset to my established reputation. Yet I came here to escape judging eyes. All I've done since I've arrived is hide from confrontation and uncomfortable conversations—I barely even talk to my father anymore.

"I won't tell anyone," I promise. "Not without your consent."

Velma relaxes at this. She slowly returns to me, letting me hug her under the cover of the awning. I press a light kiss to her forehead, memorizing the moment.

She tilts her face up, her lips ghosting mine so softly it's hard not to claim them again, but I know I have to let her be in control of this. "I've wanted to do that for so long," she admits quietly. "Kiss you, I mean. I've thought about how to do it. I've imagined and forecast so many different ways it could happen, but then I thought the host got you. I thought— I couldn't wait any longer."

"I've been in life-threatening danger in your presence before," I remind her, Sarah Ravencroft's unholy laugh echoing in my mind.

"That was before I knew you," Velma tries to reason. "Before we became friends. Before there was a possibility I could actually keep you."

"I'd like it if you kept me."

She doesn't speak, just smiles softly, still close enough that I can feel more than see the muscles of her face move to do so.

"At least we picked out pumpkins before the host arrived," she says, eventually stepping back. "How about a night of jack-o'-lantern carving?" She loops her pinkie with mine, an olive branch.

I'm almost feeling better—despite Velma putting more distance between us as we return to the gang—until opening the door of the Mystery Machine reveals that Shaggy's pumpkin haul has also rotted, despite being out of the patch before the specter arrived.

160

CHAPTER TWENTY

The Harvest Host hits two more locations in the following days. The fact that I was nowhere near either has not made a difference to my reputation at school, so I've begun eating lunch in the library to avoid prying and angry eyes. What used to be whispers and sidelong glances have turned into jeers and hateful glares. Technically, I don't have to hide today. Jordan hasn't been seen all day. The rest of the student body isn't as hive-minded without her vindictive leadership. But I don't want to risk it.

It's a small reprieve that's made even better when Velma joins me.

The specter has hit enough locations to isolate a pattern. It almost always shows up in the late afternoon to early evening. With that knowledge and several possible locations already visited, the gang has narrowed the potential targets down to only two locations: the garden in front of the Coolsonian Museum and the Poppenbacher corn farm.

The Harvest Host seems to like locations with a lot of potential victims—the one outlier is the nursery, which it hit after closing—so the museum is most likely the next place it will visit.

"You didn't have to join me today," I tell Velma. "We're going to the museum tomorrow. I wouldn't blame you if you wanted to go back to the others to prep."

"I'm fine where I am," she says. She retrieves a large rolled-up map of the town from her backpack and shakes it open on the floor in front of us. Digging back in for her annotation tools, she also pulls out a small bag of gummy bears. She drops it in my lap. "They're vegan. I triple-checked."

Her eyes linger on my lips as I taste test the gummy bears. "Thank you," I say.

She nods repeatedly as she looks away from me. "It was no trouble," she replies, exhaling a deep breath with the words.

I set the gummy bears aside as a reward for finishing my tofu bowl. I stick out a boot-clad foot to keep one of the corners of Velma's map from rolling up. She mutters a thank-you while she places books on the other edges to weigh them down. She reaches for my copy of *Crystal & Gold*, but I stop her.

"I'm reading that one," I say.

"You are?" she asks. I scoff in false indignation, flipping open the book to where my folded math homework is marking my place.

"You bought it for me," I remind her. "What did you expect me to do with it? Wallpaper my room?"

"Well," she says. "You really hate that color . . ."

I playfully kick her hand with my outstretched foot, then pull it back so she can secure that corner of the map without my leg in the way. "See if I share these gummy bears with you now."

It's for the best that I have something to keep me occupied while she highlights potential evacuation routes and the best place to lead the Harvest Host into a trap. Reading is a lot safer than poking at the elephant in the room, the secret that keeps lightly touching my hand to point out anomalies on the map before us.

It's the first time we've been alone together since she kissed me at the pumpkin patch, but neither of us has brought that up. Velma's laser focus on the task at hand is how I know she's a certified genius, because my brain is incapable of thinking about anything but how close she's sitting to me. I've only caught her looking at me when she thought I wasn't paying attention twice, but she's had to repeat several things to me that went in one ear and out the other while I got lost in her eyes.

I try to focus on refamiliarizing myself with the chapter I left off on, about Laura and Levi Coolidge's journey to the land that would eventually become Coolsville.

The founders of Coolsville almost didn't make it to California. Their Manifest Destiny wagon train was fraught with difficulty and tragedy after tragedy. Some of those not lost to illness earlier in the trip fell due to injuries from a freak livestock stampede; later, three wagons exploded from mispacked gunpowder. Many of the pioneers feared they had been cursed. They felt haunted, not metaphorically but literally, by those they lost on the trail. This superstition spread far outside their small caravan of fortune seekers.

Several families following the same path as the Coolidge train chose to redirect after learning of the trials that had befallen them. Though it added to their travel time, they switched to the more southern trail, leading them directly to what would become Crystal Cove. This path was not without its own difficulties (as discussed in chapter 7).

After losing his first wife and both his children on the journey, Levi Coolidge latched onto the steadfast Laura Ruby, another migrant who had split from her group. She was undaunted by the superstitious gossip that kept most of the other pioneers from interacting or trading with the supposedly doomed Coolidge train. Her support invigorated Levi. Together they founded Coolsville with the surviving

members of the expedition, swearing to them that nothing
terrible would ever haunt the town.

"Did you know this?" I ask Velma. I show her the page
instead of summarizing it, knowing she can read faster than
I'd be able to explain it.

"That sounds correct," she confirms. She turns back to
the map. "So it doesn't mention what happened to Laura
Ruby's original wagon train?"

I skim the rest of the page and the next, then flip forward
a few pages to check. "No," I say. "It starts to go into settler
politics after this."

Velma looks up again. Her glasses have slid to the end
of her button nose, so I lightly push them back into place as
she looks at the pages I've just inspected. "Huh," she says.
"Interesting take on gold rush greed and colonialism. You'll
have to loan this one to me when you finish."

"Of course," I promise. "But what's it leaving out about
Laura Ruby?"

"From what I've read, her train was even worse off than
the Coolidge one," Velma explains. "She was one of only
a handful of people on her expedition to make it as far as
she did before merging with the Coolidge train. That book
makes it sound like it was a mutual decision to team up for
strength, but the Ruby train didn't really have any other
options. The other expeditions were avoiding them for the
same reason they were avoiding Levi's group."

"I wish the book went into that," I say. "I love ancient

gossip that has nothing to do with me. Give me that historical drama."

Velma laughs. "I'll keep that in mind when I pick the next book to give you."

I return to my reading and let her get back to work. The more I read, the more I question whether the Coolidges would hate me after all. I empathize deeply with the pain in their past they were trying to move on from. I know now that the early days of Coolsville were not all that rosy. Maybe if I can overcome my own painful journey, my life here could become better too. This change in my relationship with Velma has already made each day more bearable, even if we have to hide it for now.

As we finish up lunch, Velma says she thinks we're right to focus on the museum. "I think it will be the next larger target. The host may hit elsewhere first, but the museum will have more potential victims, so I think we stand the best chance of catching it there and protecting others."

I offer her the final gummy bear. When she takes it from my palm, I close my hand around hers for a second, squeezing it before letting go. The phantom of her touch remains. I wish I could keep it there.

"What are you going to do if I can't perform the spell correctly this time?" I ask.

"I'm sure you can," Velma says as she holds the library door open for me.

"It doesn't feel the way it did before," I admit to the grass yellowing between cracks in the concrete walkway. Magic used to comfort me, but now it just reminds me of the fear I felt while we fought Sarah Ravencroft's ghost and the pain of everything that came after.

Once she confirms we're alone, Velma slips her arm around my waist in a comforting half hug. "Anything can be distorted for evil," she says, "but it was *you* who saved Oakhaven. You saved the Hex Girls. You saved all of us."

It was also me who brought the destruction here. "Their evil must have followed me," I say, finally voicing my biggest fear out loud.

"That doesn't make much sense," Velma says as we walk away from the library. "Ben Ravencroft was Sarah's descendant. He was only able to summon her from her spell book because of that bloodline. You're not related to the Ravencrofts, so how could their ill intent follow you here?"

"You're right," I say, pretending I'm reassured. But even Velma has to know that there is no logical explanation why the host would claim me if it had nothing to do with my past.

"Besides, the results of my experiment still aren't ready," Velma says. "We haven't eliminated the impossible yet. The Harvest Host could have nothing at all to do with magic. We'll prove your innocence. We just need a little more time."

We don't have more time.

CHAPTER TWENTY-ONE

A scream echoes across the campus louder than the closing lunch bell.

Students ignore the call to return to class to seek the source. The screams increase in number as Velma and I race toward the noise. There's something even worse in the sound than when the Harvest Host first appeared. These are not cries of fear or fleeing. These are cries of shock and agony. Despair.

As we close in on the crowd and I recognize the location,

I feel as if my lunch may return on the spot. Teenagers are surrounding the site of the first attack, the student garden and greenhouse. Even as the faces grow more tear-streaked and terrified, something primal inside me knows that the Harvest Host hasn't returned to the scene of the crime.

"It's your fault," someone says, even though I'm the last of dozens to arrive. "She was just trying to warn us about you."

I open my mouth to ask what they're talking about, then quickly seal it as the angry crowd parts to reveal a horrific sight. Spray-painted across the frosted greenhouse roof in bronze metallic letters is a warning: SHE DESTROYED ONE TOWN. Or at least, that's what I think it's supposed to say. The last word trails off in a dripping splatter after the letter O.

Jordan, the clear perpetrator, never finished it.

What she left behind instead is far worse.

Her body rests in a cruel arc on top of the garden trellis, impaled through the stomach by the sharp metal points. There's paint on her hands, glowing gold in the sunlight. She's long gone, but her eyes lock on her target—me— in death as they did in life. Still accusing, even from the beyond.

"Witch," the voices around me echo.

"She must have just slipped," Velma says, her voice shaking as she attempts to reason with the crowd. "This area is cordoned off by police tape. Maybe someone shouted at her to get out and it startled her." She tries to get the crowd to disperse, but no one moves until teachers arrive.

My classmates cling to any authoritative adult, lobbing accusations at me even though this was obviously a freak accident. Jordan clearly fell from the greenhouse roof.

As police sirens pierce the cries and questions are shouted around us, the teachers shepherd the witnesses toward the auditorium to be interviewed by the police.

I let the crowd carry me along, because I don't know where to go next. I can't bring myself to sit down as if Jordan's death is a show I'm here to enjoy, despite how everyone is looking at me like I commissioned it myself. But I don't want to sit on the stage either. I won't lean against any of the walls we both waited at during the talent show auditions. I see her in every corner of the room.

With her hand at the small of my back, Velma guides me to sit on the carpet behind the last row of seats. She pulls out her phone and texts someone while I sit there and wait for my life to end.

I almost want the cops to accuse me like Sheriff Jones did after the Harvest Host's first appearance, because the guilt I feel is even more painful now and it has nowhere to go. It is somehow worse to watch as the officers defend me and try to defuse my crying classmates. Vandalism and pranks are one thing, but the Coolsville Police Department won't let an accusation of murder gain traction when the truth is simple.

Jordan's death is nothing more than a tragic accident.

She was so mean to me. She turned the entire school against me, probably motivated by fear our band might outshine hers at a talent show that will now most likely be canceled. Petty. Unnecessary. Nothing worth dying over.

The truth spreads among the student body the longer I sit here without handcuffs on my wrists, but that doesn't put me at ease. Jordan died because I came to Coolsville. She died warning everyone I'm dangerous, and I'm not sure she's wrong. Nothing bad had ever happened here before I arrived. This town is literally so perfect an entire book was written about it.

I may not go to prison, but the Harvest Host could show up and take back everything it has said about me in front of everyone right now and it wouldn't make a difference in the town's opinion of me.

I think about Ben Ravencroft, back before his true colors were exposed, and how he made all of us feel so sad for the legacy that had followed his ancestor Sarah. I'd thought it tragic, that centuries ago a woman seeking to help people was labeled a monster simply because people couldn't understand the knowledge behind her attempts to heal what ailed them.

I don't think it matters in the end, that Sarah truly was as evil as Oakhaven had painted her to be for tourist income. I think the bad reputation would have stayed even if her ghost had been kind and peaceful.

Once you've been branded with a scarlet letter, it's yours forever. I was naive to believe that leaving Oakhaven would save me.

Velma scoots closer to me, squeezing my hand in the hidden space between us to comfort me in secrecy. I suddenly see her apprehension about anyone finding out about us in a new light. She's right to be afraid. She shouldn't want to be associated with me. This time, I'm the one who pulls my hand out of hers and moves away. I feel clammy and lightheaded as I start walking toward the exit, like I suddenly caught the flu.

Velma follows me, asking if I'm okay, but before she can finish her question Dusk enters the auditorium.

She already knows. I can tell by the tears on her face. I know Dusk was friends with Jordan—or at least on good terms because of the class they had together. Being angry at her for finding companionship feels so stupid now, but I'm not sure how to tell her that. I don't know how to apologize without making things worse.

If Dusk thinks I did it . . . Every inch of me feels as if it's rotting like the plants in the garden. I swallow so much bile it feels like I'm chugging from a water fountain.

Dusk walks toward me. "I heard what happened. I told her—" She cuts off, choked. "I begged her to lay off you, but she got even madder after you and I fought. After we stopped speaking. I know it looks bad, but I promise she wasn't evil. She didn't deserve . . . this."

I understand. I want to tell her as much. I want to hug her and make things better between us, before it's too late. I want so many things, but when I open my mouth all that comes out is vomit.

CHAPTER TWENTY-TWO

When the Mystery Machine starts to pull into the museum parking lot the next day, Fred spins around in a U-turn so rushed it nearly topples us over. "My dad is here," he says tensely as we drive out the way we just came in.

I cup my hands against the tinted back window. I guess we weren't the only ones to have figured out the host's pattern and potential next target. The view is clear, even as it rapidly shrinks with distance: The museum's garden is swarming with cops. We definitely can't park there. The van's bold colors aren't exactly inconspicuous. Yet another thing to add to my list of reasons Goth Is Good. A black van would stand a much better chance of not being spotted.

The sheer number of cops is surprising, though. The police have certainly been annoyed by the other incidents, but this is an intense preventative turnout.

"Must be because of Jordan," Velma says from the passenger seat. That makes sense. A death—even if only tangentially related to the host—makes things infinitely more urgent. I was allowed to go home earlier than the other students yesterday after literally puking in shock, so I wasn't there for the aftermath. I didn't see much before I left anyway.

This morning, Velma told me that reporters stationed themselves at the school soon after I left, using Jordan's death to spread the paranoia about the Harvest Host, even after the police officially ruled Jordan's death an accident. I don't even want to think about how the reporters would have treated me if I'd still been at the school, or how I would have responded to questioning. All that's been in my head is the image of Jordan's corpse, toppled like the statue on my first day—it's overtaken everything else.

The gang offered to let me sit out this sting, but I want this to be over. I *need* this to end. No one else deserves to be harmed by this monster and whatever it wants from me.

I lower myself back to the floor of the van. Scooby pants at me from the dog hammock securing him in the second row of seats. Shaggy's watching me too.

"You're sure you're okay back there?" he asks. "I could have made room for you."

I nod, even though a toolbox is digging into my hip and my feet are falling asleep. I listen as Daphne comforts Fred since his dad's presence has stressed him out. He was already anxious about today after the failure at the pumpkin patch.

"Do you think he broke into my room to find our maps?" he asks. Daphne just sighs, as if knowing she can't honestly assure him that Fred Jones Sr. wouldn't betray his privacy. Scooby whines from the tension filling the van.

"I told him that Thorn has nothing to do this!" he says. "He doesn't care about real detective work, Daph. He goes for the obvious answer every single time, even when—" Fred cuts his own rant off with a frustrated exhale. "I could actually help him if he'd listen to me. He still sees me as a toddler pretending I can read his paperwork. Everything I say is nonsense to him."

"I know," Daphne says. "He won't face the truth until he has no other choice. But *we're* listening."

"We believe you, Fred," Shaggy says. Velma nods.

"I'm grateful for your help," I tell Fred as we pull into an emptier parking lot. "All of your help. It means a lot that you guys are working so hard to prove my innocence, despite everything that's happened. I'm really sorry it's causing you problems at home."

Fred laughs bitterly. "Thorn, you are not the root of my issues with my dad," he says with a sigh. "Don't worry about that, at the very least."

He parks the Mystery Machine behind the museum, in the lot of a bar that isn't open for the evening yet. A family is exiting the museum through the back entrance and Velma hurries forward to catch the door. We follow her inside before it shuts and locks. My phone says it's 5:00. The museum closes at six.

"Friday I'm in Love" by the Cure plays on the overhead speakers. I mouth the lyrics to soothe myself as we attempt to blend in with the crowd. We creep toward the front of the museum, past a large T. rex skull and an exhibit on the gold mines that helped the town gain its early wealth. At the top of a staircase to the second floor, we peer out a floor-to-ceiling window at the large garden below.

"I knew it," Fred says.

The police are patrolling the garden, which is the size of a football field, but they aren't looking at the sky for the Harvest Host or at the ground for its mist. Their eyes are on the very parking lot we narrowly avoided parking in.

They're not looking for the host. They're looking for me.

I step away from the window. Does proving the truth even matter anymore? I'm afraid that even if I can conjure the magic we need to stop the host, my reputation will be as irreparably destroyed in Coolsville as it was in Oakhaven. "What do we do now?" I ask.

"We stick to the plan," Daphne says. She tilts Fred's face from his dejected watch with a single finger on his chin. "Right?"

Fred sniffs. "Right," he says. "We stick to the plan.

Everyone knows their stations?" We all agree.

We follow him back to the ground floor. We split up there to look less conspicuous, boys to the west wing and girls to the east to cover more ground at exhibits near the entrance and with a view of the garden. In a less crowded hall, I settle between an exhibit honoring the Coolidges and a plaque stating that this section of the museum was generously donated by the Blake Family Trust.

"Is that your family?" I ask Daphne.

She grimaces at the plaque. "No," she says quickly. "I mean, yes, but it's not as big of a deal as it looks. I, uh, I have to go to the bathroom." She takes off before I can apologize, though I'm not sure how I'd begin. *Sorry for reminding you of your family's immense wealth?* That would make everything a lot more chill, I'm sure.

I meander in the direction of the Coolidge exhibit, even though it's the last place I want to go. I don't need any more reminders of how I'm everything this town despises, but I guess we all have pasts we want to escape.

Maybe Daphne's discomfort with her nepo baby status is why she's so understanding of my own shame. It definitely seems to be one of the things that bond her and Fred. They both want to avoid becoming their parents, Fred constantly testing the boundaries of the law to investigate and Daphne dedicated to being generous with her time and friendship rather than flaunting money for attention.

I duck in next to Velma at to a display with flipping true-or-false questions about Coolsville's pioneer days. I'm certain she's played this game during an earlier visit to the museum and likely has every answer memorized, but she still looks at me with a proud grin after silently confirming her answer. The fingers of her free hand lightly brush mine as she flips another question open.

"How do your parents feel about what you and your friends do?" I ask Velma. I've never met her family—or any of the gang's except Fred's dad—but she always talks fondly about how proud of her they are. I know the Dinkleys aren't as well-off as the Blakes are, but Velma's parents value her education as much as she does and have worked really hard to make sure cost is never a barrier to her ambitious goals.

"They're supportive," she says, flipping the final true-or-false question closed. She does a cursory sweep out the window, checking for any changes. "They think these 'little puzzles we find for ourselves' will make for unique college essays."

"So they think it's temporary," I say. "A phase you're going through." I shimmy my shoulders, framing my face with my hands. "Never heard that one before."

"My abuela keeps telling them that 'if she keeps her head stuffed with books and mysteries she'll never find a man.'" She quotes her grandmother's warning in a thick but affectionate accent.

"Is that what you want?" I ask. Velma's brows furrow with confusion. "Do you want to find a man?" I clarify. "Ultimately? It's okay if you do. Or if you're not sure."

She breaks eye contact, but doesn't immediately answer

yes or no. It's the closest we've come to talking about our kiss at the pumpkin patch since it happened. After another look around the room, she says, "I know what I want." Nothing else.

I'm almost grateful to be overwhelmed by our current mission. If I weren't bubbling with anxiety about what we'll do if the mist shows up, that casual statement would probably earn a spiral of its own. Maybe this is one of the reasons the gang loves investigating mysteries. Existential concerns like "What are we?" kind of have to take a back seat during a supernatural stakeout.

Velma slips her phone out of her pocket. "The host still isn't here yet," she says, changing the topic. She shows me her phone screen. The group chat confirms that no one else has spotted the toxic party crasher either. The museum closes in fifteen minutes.

Velma frowns at her phone, focus turned to texting with the others. It will be another somber drive home if we strike out. She was certain it would hit here next. Unless it surprises us within the next ten minutes, the Harvest Host will have lost the majority of its potential swath of victims.

"Should we come back tomorrow?" I ask.

"I don't know yet," Velma admits, "but we should probably leave now."

We reunite with the rest of the gang at the giant dinosaur skull and try to exit the way we came, but we're turned away by museum staff. They've already secured that section of the building for the evening. We have no choice but to leave through the front entrance. Past the garden. Past the entire police squadron.

We do a decent job of blending in with the crowd at first, but something catches my eyes—a quick flash of gold light—and in the short pause I take to focus on it I lose the gang. Other late-leavers shoulder past me, testing my balance on the cobblestones. Someone grabs me and pulls me from the rush, but when I look up to thank them my gratitude vanishes.

It's not one of my friends or a kind stranger. It's Sheriff Jones.

His grip on my arm is so tight, I have no choice but to follow him into the garden and farther away from escape. The sky is still clear, showing no sign of the host's potential arrival. I'm clammy, but I can't tell if it's nervous sweat or spray from some watering drones going up and down the length of the greenery.

"Ms. McKnight, we keep being called to the same places," Fred Jones Sr. points out. "Interesting, isn't it? Why is it that you have been found at every sighting of this 'Harvest Host'—"

"I wasn't at either of the last two locations," I interrupt. "I have alibis. You can ask your son."

Maybe bringing up Fred was a low blow, but at least it works. Sheriff Jones lets go of my arm with a shove and shakes his hand as if to shed my delinquency from his skin. "Alibis, yeah," he says. "You've got plenty of those. It would almost be funny, if there was anything amusing about these situations you keep placing yourself in. May I remind you that someone is dead."

"I know that," I say.

He leans in, towering over me as he reclaims the space he just put between us. "You'd already be in a jail cell if I could prove your alibi false, but that would make my son an accessory," he snarls, his voice an angry whisper. "You're a bad influence. My Fred would have nothing to do with this scandal if it weren't for you. Now I have to explain to my superiors why my child is a repeat witness."

I bite my lip until blood blossoms on my tongue. I can't tell him the truth, despite how badly I want to. That Mystery Inc. basically dragged me to every location I was caught at. That his precious little boy and his friends seem dead set on defining themselves as the opposite of the town motto, no matter the consequences.

My silence doesn't shut him up. "You clearly take after your mother's side of the family," he says. "That Ravencroft bloodline is nothing but bad news."

"What?" I say. "My mom wasn't a Ravencroft."

The sheriff calls over one of his lackeys, who's standing by the thinning herd of museum visitors, a clipboard with a file attached in his hand. The file looks like the one his coworkers confronted Dad and me with at home, but it's a lot thicker now. The police have been investigating, just not the host.

Sheriff Jones flips through the folder until he finds what he's looking for. It's a printout from a fan site for Ben

183

Ravencroft's horror novels, discussing the little that's known about his family history. *Ben was always intentionally quiet about his family,* the article reads, *but we've uncovered some high school photos in a former classmate's yearbook!*

There's one of him and a girl who looks heart-stoppingly familiar. The caption reads *Siblings Benjamin and Jennifer Ravencroft participate in a chess tournament together.*

I would have recognized her even if the photo were black-and-white, but the color printout doesn't dull her bright green eyes. The ones she gave me.

It's my mother.

CHAPTER TWENTY-THREE

A friendly face finally finds the sheriff and me, but it's too late.

"Dad!" Fred yells from the border of the garden, held back by his father's lackeys. "Let her go! Leave her alone!"

Sheriff Jones turns from me. His face grows red.

He stalks toward his rebellious son, leaving me unattended. Fred continues to cause a scene, yelling at and goading his father, but his eyes are on me. I know Mystery Inc. well enough now to recognize this as a diversion. The others are nowhere to be seen. I could win money betting that the van is idling nearby, waiting for me to make a break for it.

I'm not playing along.

I use the commotion Fred's gifted me to escape the garden unseen, but I don't regroup with the others like I know he wants me to.

I walk myself home.

The sheriff was right to suspect me all along. Everything that's happened is my fault. I brought Ben and Sarah's evil magic to Coolsville. But it didn't latch onto me when I used her spell book. It was inside me the entire time.

These thoughts plague me as I walk. It takes hours to get home, the navigation app draining my battery to exhaustion two streets from my house. By the time I get back, it's so late even my father has given up on waiting for me. The kitchen is empty. Not even a note.

I drag myself up to the pink room and plug my phone in, the only responsibility I can manage before curling up in bed and crying myself to sleep.

The morning brings no solace. I turn on my phone to dozens of concerned texts, the most disappointing one confirming that the Harvest Host hit the museum after all—in the middle of the night, after the cops ended their patrol.

Velma texts me privately, outside of the group chat:

> **Velma:** Fred told us what his dad said. It doesn't change anything. Not for me.

I don't agree. My restless dreams last night were of nothing but Oakhaven after Sarah Ravencroft was banished back into her spell book. After my *uncle* was banished with her, swallowed up in the tome by the words I spoke. I should have known then. Velma said I was the only one who could do it because my magic was pure, but Ben Ravencroft was only able to summon Sarah in the first place because of the direct ancestral line.

My success wasn't a triumph of good over evil. It was the beginning of the end. Oakhaven was already razed by the time I spoke the incantation. The place that built me scorched into ruins. Now I'm destroying another innocent town.

The book should have swallowed me up, too.

"Sally?" Dad asks hopefully at the door. He opens it without knocking. "You're home," he breathes, unable to hide the relief in his voice. I feel him settle on the edge of my bed. "You're running late today. I can have breakfast ready in a few minutes, but you'll need to hurry to make it to school on time."

"I'm not going," I say from under the covers.

"Are you sick?" he asks.

"I can never go back," I say. "I can't go anywhere ever again."

He peels my duvet from my face. His weathered palm

caresses my forehead, the caregiver in him on high alert. "You don't have a fever."

"It's in my blood," I say. "I'm cursed. Why didn't you tell me?" I drag myself to a sitting position against the headboard. I want to look him in the eyes when he lies to me yet again, like he's done my whole life. "Why?" I ask, my voice shattered by my pain. "Why didn't you tell me I have Ravencroft blood?"

"Oh, darling," he says, dejected but not surprised.

"Is that why you didn't fight the move?" I ask. "You were so easy to convince. Were you afraid the truth would come out back home?"

"Sally," he says, "I didn't want you to feel this way. Your mother didn't either. She was estranged from her brother. They had very different opinions on how to use magic, and it drove them apart. It was her choice, long before you were born. I didn't know the depth of their divide until Ben showed his true colors that awful night. Your mother only told me their relationship could not be salvaged. She couldn't walk the path he was following."

"You had no right to keep it a secret from me," I try to bite out angrily, but my voice breaks again.

My dad stands. The same hand that checked my forehead with such concern clenches tight at the back of his neck. "I know," he admits. "I should have told you sooner. The tourist scheme . . . I knew it was wrong. I knew you'd be upset if—*when* you found out, and your mother would have hated it."

"She's not here!" I snap. "You can't make decisions that affect my entire life based on what she told you sixteen years ago."

"Don't," Dad says. "Please, baby girl, I never planned on doing this alone. Jenny was always the one destined to be a parent. Just . . . give me a minute."

He leaves my room. I stay put, unsure what to do now.

A part of me hoped, wished, dreamed that he would respond to my accusation with bafflement. That he would say the cops lied. It was all a mistake. He'd pull me into his arms and Daddy would fix everything. I'd be okay.

I start crying again, the second time in twelve hours. The dried smears of my unwashed mascara from the night before grow wet again, ink flooding my cheeks and clouding my vision. My dad looks like just another dark blob when he returns. I can't tell he's real until he wipes away my tears and tucks me under his arm.

"Don't fret, honey," my father says, misunderstanding the cause of my crying. "I didn't go anywhere. I just had to grab something for you." He brushes more tears from my eyes and kisses my forehead, tickling me with the whiskers of his cropped beard. "Your mother loved you so much," he says. "She was so excited to raise you with me. I hope you know that."

"I know," I say. I've never doubted her love for me, even with only secondhand memories to go by. That's what makes this so much worse.

"She was the epitome of what the Ravencroft name

should have stood for. A long history of people who cared deeply about each other and the earth." I nod against his chest, but he can tell I'm not entirely convinced. He lets go of me and places a wooden box with a worn metal latch in my lap.

Like clockwork, I flash back to Sarah's spell book, but the contents of this box aren't teeming with negative energy. Pressed flowers and small baby food jars repurposed into herb containers surround a hand-bound journal.

"I'll give you some alone time with your mom," Dad says. He gives me one last kiss on the cheek and leaves.

I pick up one of the jars. Inside, a chunk of black quartz is peppered with the remnants of what looks like nettle and bay leaf. In flowing script on faded sticker paper placed over the old label, my mother inscribed: *Protection Spell for Sweet Sally.* The other jars contain similar contents and promises: *Happiness Hopes for My Daughter. Love-Strengthening Spell for Simon. Healing Spell for Ben.*

I untie the knot sealing the journal. It flips open effortlessly, stuffed to the brim with unattached papers that spill across my bedspread. The journal lies flat, too heavy once opened to close upon itself without help.

I tug it closer, reading the first handwritten entry I come across, dated a few months before I was born:

Ben called me again today. He heard about the baby. It was hard talking to him, because he was so excited by the idea of becoming an uncle. I haven't figured out how to tell him I won't let him see her. I can't. Not if he stays committed to this dangerous theory about our ancestor Sarah.

The way he talks about her scares me. He's shown me proof of her misdeeds. It doesn't shame him the way it does me. It excites him. He's angry at our family, the centuries-long effort to clear the Ravencroft name. I don't understand it. He used to be my best friend. ~~I loved~~ I love him. I wish he would come back to the light.

He's such a good writer. I don't think he believes me when I tell him so. I don't know if this growing obsession stems from doubt in his talent. Maybe writing horror isn't enough for him. Maybe putting terror into words doesn't exorcise his fears the way he needs. I hope he finds the healing he deserves. I know that seeking to control the dark will never work.

I spend the rest of the morning and much of the afternoon reading my mother's diary entries. The main focus is notes on spells and observations about her Wicca practice. Through her writing, I am reminded that there's so much more to Wicca—and magic—than what a lot of people believe. It's not a binary split between good and evil. Witchcraft isn't simply one or the other; in fact, it's individual to the person practicing it. What happened in Oakhaven didn't destroy just my reputation but also my belief in Wicca, in who I was.

I forgot what I had previously known about Wicca, letting what others assumed replace my lived experiences in the aftermath of the disaster.

But I don't have to fear what lies in me as long as my intentions are good. My mother believed magic would empower me to help myself and the world. She wrote often about how much she wanted to teach me that herself. Neither of us knew it would take this long for me to learn these lessons.

As school lets out for the day and my phone once again lights up with concerned texts from my friends, I unpin a spell from my mother's journal and boot up the navigation app once again. This time for directions to the Poppenbacher corn farm—the only place left on Mystery Inc.'s list that the Harvest Host hasn't hit yet.

CHAPTER TWENTY-FOUR

The Poppenbacher farm is empty when I arrive. It's a private farm, so I wasn't expecting a crowd, but I'm relieved not to spot a gun-toting owner scouting for trespassers. Still, I crouch low as I race toward the towering cornstalks.

The earth is brown, the plants a natural gold, no trace of the toxic green to be seen. I pause for a second, closing my eyes and taking a deep breath. Feeling the cool air blow through my hair, I root myself to the moment and focus on my intention.

"Earth below, sky above," I say, repeating the words I found in my mother's journal. I'd spent the trip here memorizing them so I could say the spell from my heart. "Heal this harvest with my love. Take my hands and let me toil, protect tonight this bountiful soil."

The spell shows no signs of taking effect. In fact, it's the opposite: Green mist starts to slither out of the wall of cornstalks. I look to the sky for the host, but I'm still alone. It hasn't arrived yet. Maybe I still have a chance.

I drop to my knees and shove my hands in the soil, trying not to panic. "Earth below, sky above," I recite, gripping roots between my fingers. "Heal this harvest with my love." I dig my hands in deeper until I can't see my wrists anymore, putting all I have into the spell. "Take my hands and let me toil, protect tonight this bountiful soil."

The fog thickens.

"What are you doing now, little witch?" I'm not surprised to hear the Harvest Host's voice taunting me. I don't need to look up to know it's above me. It blocks out the setting sun, making my position feel even more vulnerable. My hands are buried deep in the ground, and the green mist is beginning to impair my vision.

I will not leave these plants to die. I will *not* give up.

But it's getting harder to breathe. My hands leave the soil like an undead soul clawing out of a grave, and I crawl with the same mindless shuffling directly into the cornfield. I drag myself through the dirt, the bottoms of the stalks becoming harder to see as the mist continues to rise around me. Once I can't see in any direction anymore, I stand up and begin to run, praying I'm heading the right way—wherever that may be. It's more of a struggle to stay upright than it should be; the fog is making me lightheaded with every step in the decaying soil.

The fog is nearly to my thighs now, and even with death forming rapidly on the stalks around me, I still can't find my way out. If I don't get to the other side of the field before the mist engulfs me, nothing will be able to save me. The other victims recovered because they got medical attention quickly. No one knows I'm here. I'll be long dead before anyone even realizes I'm missing.

It's hard to run through a cornfield on a good day. With the crops rotting, bending, and dissolving in every direction—left, right, up, down—I keep tripping.

I can hear the host's laugh hovering above me. I'm not going to make it.

I fall again, but this time my attempts to right myself fail as the stalks I grab for help melt to mush in my hands. I roll onto my back and see the host is right there, blocking out any last gulps of fresh air I might have been able to take. It doesn't say anything this time as it descends on me. There's no point in taunting me now that I have no way out. I close my eyes as the host lowers. *Is it going to eat me?* I wonder. *Can it even do that?*

Closing my eyes doesn't erase my terror. I wonder if Jordan had enough time to be afraid in her short fall from the greenhouse roof. My mind conjures an image of my corpse on the dark canvas of my eyelids. I rot from the inside out, just like the plants. I'll lie here, crystallized atop my failure. That's how they'll find me, so freshly gone I could almost be sleeping, but when they touch me my skin will bruise like a mushy apple. I'll break open, intestines splitting open with grime, and no one will be able to seal me shut again. The tainted soil will claim what's left of me.

I wasn't strong enough. The host's menacing cackle will be the last thing I ever hear.

"Hey! Over here!" a voice calls out.

. . . *Velma?*

I open my eyes just in time to see an arrow pierce the host. It doesn't fall, but it flickers and fades a bit like it did at the pumpkin patch. Only this time it doesn't recover. One of its cavernous eyes and part of its mouth are almost fully gone. It looks like a smashed jack-o'-lantern.

"Thorn!" Velma cries. She breaks through the decaying corn. I sit up only to lose my balance as she gathers me into her arms, dragging me into a hug with more strength than I would have thought someone as tiny as her was capable of. "I was so worried," she says. "I thought we were too late. Come on, we have to go."

She helps me stand. Hand in hand, we resume our escape. "East!" Fred yells from somewhere in the field. "The mist hasn't gotten there yet!" Velma pivots and heads in a different direction despite not having a compass on her. Not for the first time, I find myself in awe of Mystery Inc.'s team unity. As we run, we're joined by Shaggy, Scooby, and

Daphne, who is wielding an actual scythe.

As Daphne takes the lead to clear the way, I notice a large black object in Scooby's mouth. But I don't have time to ask about it. The host is still chasing us, more visible now with Daphne clearing the obscuring stalks around us. It has stopped saying anything intelligible, but it's still making sounds. It's almost like white noise from a sleep machine, except not soothing in the slightest.

"I think they know we caught one," Shaggy says.

"I think you're right," Velma agrees. I'm even more confused.

We break out of the field just before Fred does. He's armed like Daphne, but with a crossbow instead of the most morbid of farm tools. I must look just as slack-jawed about it, because he says, "I'm on the school archery team!" as if that explains everything. But I'm forced to let it go since we still aren't clear of the host, and the fog rising from the rot has overtaken the entire field. It's still spreading. We'll suffocate if we stay here.

CHAPTER TWENTY-FIVE

"Follow me!" Fred yells, pointing his crossbow to an open grain silo. "We can hide in there!"

He runs in first and waits until we are all inside before closing the silo door tight. Of all the places to get stuck fleeing from a fog monster, this is a decent option. A halo of lights are installed at the top of the narrow cylinder and the amount of corn isn't too overwhelming. It's barely ankle-high in most places.

Realizing anyone could notice our entwined fingers

now, I start to let go of Velma's hand, but she only squeezes tighter.

No one is looking at us anyway. Scooby drops the item in his mouth and coughs, running his tongue against the roof of his mouth repeatedly as if trying to wash out a bad taste. I let go of Velma's hand to inspect the object. It's heavy and clearly broken, but the GreenGrove logo is still visible despite all the dog drool.

"It's a drone," Velma explains. She reaches down and breaks off a weirdly shaped lump attached to the top of the drone. She tinkers with it until a light flashes on and then the host's missing eye socket and broken smile project on the silo wall. "GreenGrove attached lights to their watering drones and used that and the mist to create the Harvest Host illusion. I'm sure another drone has a speaker that the voice came out."

"So the specter was a fake?" I ask. "A company made this. . . . But why? What kind of lawn care company *kills* healthy plants?"

"You may have noticed how hard this start-up has been pitching itself to businesses around Coolsville," Velma says. "They wanted to corner the market here; they even have a bid in for a citywide contract. But they didn't do enough testing. Their new pesticide interacts with a previously harmless fungus very common in this region of California to accidentally create a toxin that's killing all the plants. That was what my experiment was about: I applied a sample of the pesticide to healthy soil and set conditions to speed up the incubation period to days instead of weeks. I just got the results this morning and would have explained them at school today if you'd shown up."

"I'm sorry," I say, but Velma shakes her head.

"I'm not mad at you," she says. "I should've told you earlier, but I wanted to make sure my hypothesis was correct before I got your hopes up."

"I get it," I say, giving her a small smile.

"My experiment proved what I began to suspect after the second visit of the host," Velma says, continuing her explanation. "The healthy sample I treated with GreenGrove's pesticide was identical to the rotted samples collected from the sites the Harvest Host had already visited. We checked the records and confirmed that every location hit was treated with the pesticide exactly two weeks before they rotted. That's why the host sometimes visited when there was no one around to scare. It couldn't control when the rot would happen. It was bound to a predetermined schedule."

"And now we have everything we need, thanks to Scoob," Shaggy adds. "Good job retrieving the drone when the arrow hit it, buddy." Scooby paws at the corn at his feet, bashful with the praise.

"We told you we'd prove your innocence," Fred says.

"I'm thankful for it," I say, meaning it, "but I'm not sure what this has to do with me. I had never heard of GreenGrove before I moved here. Why would they drag me into their mess?"

"When they discovered what they'd done, they needed

someone to take the fall," Daphne says from her place by the door. "Screwing up this majorly would have jeopardized their shot at the citywide contract and could have bankrupted the company. Start-up culture is ruthless. There's a ton of money involved and very little regulation."

"That's why they tried to blame you." Fred picks up Daphne's train of thought seamlessly, they're so perfectly in sync. "GreenGrove was probably inspired by the *Daily Babbler*'s article on your 'spooky' band moving to town and took advantage of it to frame you. As we've all seen, the tabloid coverage of the Oakhaven disaster is very easy to uncover with simple searches. It wasn't hard to build a narrative against you."

"If it could all be dismissed as cruel vandalism by the new goth girl, they would have gotten away clean," I summarize. "I understand now. It probably would have worked, too, if not for you four. And Scooby. How did you guys know I was here?"

"We didn't," Shaggy says.

"I was hoping you weren't," Velma adds. "We were simply following the clues. Poppenbacher is a suspicious old man. He only recently agreed to try the pesticide when GreenGrove offered a substantial discount. Why *are* you here?"

"I was trying magic again," I admit. "A healing spell instead of a banishing one." Velma starts to smile, but I cut her off before she can show too much pride. "It didn't work."

"It will," she says. "You just need more practice."

Scooby barks in agreement and we all laugh, until he does it again. It's a weird sound, half bark, half cough. He stands on his hind legs, leaning on Shaggy for support. They're nearly the same height like this. Shaggy holds Scooby up with both hands despite the Great Dane's weight, trying to keep him upright to protect him.

It doesn't matter that we outran the drones. Our escape wasn't really an escape at all. The corn in this silo is just as tainted as the rest. The mist has started to form in the corn piles. It's already as tall as Scooby when he's on all fours.

Fred heads to the door we came through, but the handle won't budge. "It's stuck," he says, sounding more worried than I've ever heard him.

He steps aside to let Daphne try. "No," she says. "It's locked." She pulls a pin from her hair and attempts to unlock it. "It's not working."

"It must be one of the programmers," Velma says. "Drones can't lock doors, and someone had to be controlling the host drone and feeding it lines to taunt you."

"They locked us in?" I ask.

Fred kicks the metal wall, the sound echoing throughout the silo. "I should have thought of that before," he says. "If we'd put someone on the perimeter, we could—"

"You can't get lost in the past," Daphne says, pulling him away from the wall. "We have to focus on what we can do now." She tries to cut a hole in the wall with the scythe, to no avail. Fred and Shaggy attempt storming the door, but that doesn't work either.

The mist continues to rise around us, thicker than usual in the enclosed space despite the limited grain to fuel it. I squat down, cutting off my line of sight. Velma calls out my name, but I don't let her pull me up. I run my hands along the dusty floor until my dirty fingers grasp some dead seeds. "Earth below, sky above," I choke out. "Heal this harvest with my love. Take my hands and let me toil, protect tonight this bountiful soil."

I repeat the words over and over again. I've never wanted something as badly as I do this. I focus on my intentions. I need to somehow make up for the terror this tech unleashed while using my name. I can't do that if I die in this silo.

I begin to feel the spell working. The same way I sensed the host in the orchard before it showed itself. The primal knowing I felt in the hall at school.

But then, I feel it slip away. My chest tightens like it did when I ran through the cornstalks, the mist around us casting a mental fog as well. My attempt at healing decays beneath my hands. I'm not strong enough in my Wicca practice after ignoring it for all these months.

"I'm sorry," I tell the others as I stand up. They shake their heads, dismissing my failure through wheezing breaths. Shaggy is cradling Scooby completely off the ground now to protect him from the mist. Velma moves toward me, reaching out in the densest part of the haze, only to turn away at a sudden burst of light.

Somehow, the door has opened.

We rush for the light without asking after our savior. The

fog has faded outside. I take in gulps of air while arms pull me away from the field. It takes my eyes a while to adjust to the brightness, but I'm still not prepared for the sight in front of me when my vision finally focuses.

Dusk.

Luna is there too, helping Scooby step over the rotted crops to reach safety. Dusk pats my back aggressively, encouraging me to cough out the bad air. "You solved the mystery too?" I ask once I can speak again, confused by their presence and lightheaded from the fog and exertion.

"What?" she says, "No. We were worried after you skipped school and didn't answer our texts. We used the Where Are You? Friend Finder app. You guys solved the mystery?"

"They did," I cough. "I was just trying to heal the plants." I grip her arm, squeezing tight, pleading. "I'm sorry for being so selfish. You had every reason to be upset. I was too focused on my own worries to care about yours. I should have been there for you. Please forgive me."

She pulls her forearm free from my clutch, then takes my hand in her own. "You weren't entirely wrong," she says. "You were scared and overwhelmed. We all were. I didn't mean to give away any secrets, and if I'd known how far Jordan would go, I would take it all back, if only to save her life. I just . . . I missed having someone to talk to."

"Me too," I admit. "I love you and Luna. You're my soul sisters."

"I love you too. And I don't want to lose any more friends," Dusk says.

"Never," I say, pulling her into a hug. Luna smiles at us from where she stands a few feet away, helping Daphne feed Scooby a bottle of water. "Never again," I promise.

As we separate, I try to play off the tears leaking from my eyes as a reaction to the chemicals I've been inhaling, but we know better. Dusk returns to Luna to help the rest of our friends. The final rays of the setting sun glow gold over the patch of dead grass I sit on, and despite everything, it feels like a happy ending.

I wasn't able to save us by myself, but I never had to. I always had a team behind me, even when I didn't feel like I deserved one. Even when I intentionally cut myself off from those who cared about me. Velma knew that before I did. She's always been so fearless. And maybe it's just my whipped, traitorous heart, but I could have sworn that worry was waning in her, too. I gave her the opportunity to hide from the others in the silo. She held me tighter.

Watching her stride toward me with purpose is like the oxygen I desperately need. The taste of her lips is the only medicine I want. But when she opens her mouth to speak, only coughs come out instead. "I need to tell you," she tries, legs buckling. "Important . . ." I rush forward and she collapses in my arms.

CHAPTER TWENTY-SIX

This is a waste of time.

I wish I were still at the hospital sitting by Velma's bedside, but instead I'm standing on a stage at city hall picking at the hem of the dress GreenGrove delivered to my house specifically for this event. It's a soft silk, the same forest green as their logo. "It complements your eyes," Dad said on the drive to city hall this morning. I want to set it on fire.

"We applaud the Coolsville courage of these young girls,"

the CEO of GreenGrove, Jeremy Mackey, says. "Kimberly Hale, Jane Brooks, and Sally McKnight have done this town and our fledgling company a great service in exposing the bad actors who orchestrated the 'Harvest Host' scam." He gestures at the three of us with both hands, waiting until the crowd of cherry-picked reporters and city officials takes the cue and applauds us.

I can't bring myself to look at my bandmates. We shouldn't be standing on this stage during this mockery of an apology. Luna didn't want to, but the alternative was letting GreenGrove get away with everything. Since Jordan's death was ruled a "tragic accident," no one is being formally charged or held accountable for what they did to her. Our agreeing to this meant they at least had to answer for the damage they did to the town.

After we escaped the silo, we gave the police our statements, the downed drone, and the soil samples as evidence. But there were questions we couldn't answer. It's not like we could tell the cops about the weird taunt in the school hall, not without admitting we were breaking and entering ourselves at the time. But if someone from GreenGrove had followed us to the school, why didn't they steal Velma's experiment that could implicate them? Or at the very least sabotage it?

Threads like that lingered with me, curious strings that Mystery Inc. couldn't tie up. Not without Velma, the brains of their operation. She was still unconscious when the ambulances arrived, the shortest member of our group and therefore the most exposed to the low-hanging mist.

I've spent so much time these past few days sitting next to her bedside. Watching her. Holding her hand. Wondering what the future will bring. Will she wake up? If she does, will she be okay? Will she be the same? Will she *feel* the same?

She should be on this stage instead of me. She should be the one explaining the entire dastardly plot. The rest of Mystery Inc. lurk in the back of the conference room where the event is taking place. They're as well dressed as the rest of the official attendees, and more respectful than CEO Mackey deserves.

It's not fair.

Everyone knows that the end of this torment is Mystery Inc.'s triumph, but the town they saved refuses to reward their "insubordination." New citizens proving their commitment to Coolsville by clearing their name instead of fleeing a frame job is the only story the city is willing to sell.

Coolsville has been almost too happy to switch sides. Of course this town has no monsters, people say. It has no witches. No specters. This is corruption, plain and simple. Coolsville is normal. Nothing bad happens here, even though the hospital is still swamped with people even worse off than Velma and now there's a body to bury. This isn't what I thought vindication would look like.

Innocence has a weird aftertaste. The aftermath of the Ravencrofts—of my uncle and ancestor—in Oakhaven was messy, but at least it was something. I can't fault my hometown for reacting how it did—I was struggling with how to move forward myself. A normal town, like Coolsville so desperately claims to be, would be more broken by this betrayal. They trusted GreenGrove. The Harvest Host destroyed more than crops, but people are acting as if there is nothing else to reckon with.

All I've wanted since the moment this began is a clean slate, but there is no such thing as time travel. Erasing what happened when the damage is still here is a caricature of collective duty. That fits Mackey's image. He's a caricature himself, a tall, lanky white man with long brown hair and a sharp goatee. If not for the thousand-dollar suit, he'd look more at home in a free love commune than a boardroom.

The CEO has moved on from our momentary acknowledgment to a mash-up of corporate buzzwords. Integrity. Social responsibility. His speech sounds more like a bad Notes app apology than someone truly taking accountability for poisoning dozens of townspeople.

"Environmental sustainability is a key focus in our ethical framework," he recites robotically. "That's why, to put our money where our mouth is in our promise to Coolsville, we are proud to honor these young girls with the first annual GreenGrove Sustainability Scholarship."

He pulls a sheet off a giant cardboard check positioned prominently behind us. Our full names are written in a boring script front, just above the words *five thousand dollars.*

And there it is. Buying us off.

Just like they've bought off the rest of the town. GreenGrove has paid a few thousand in fines and supposedly fired the unnamed conspirators, while promising future transparency in their pesticide formula. But I know this whole thing is a farce. Jeremy Mackey's apologies are scripted and staged, as fraudulent as this oversize check. We can't cash this at a bank. It exists to secure our carefully choreographed smiles of gratitude and forgiveness.

"Blood money," Luna snarls through clenched teeth. Her long nails pierce the bright paint where she holds the check. I've never seen her as angry as she was when this press conference was pitched to us.

"Remember," Dusk whispers, "we're doing this for them." She flashes a pageant smile for the photographer while tipping her head toward Mystery Inc. I keep my eyes locked on the gang, who convinced us not to burn the city's joint offer with GreenGrove live on the band's social media page. We wanted nothing more than to expose the entire town's complicity, but calmer heads prevailed. We could do more to help the damaged businesses by playing along than causing further problems.

So instead we're on this stage, posing as polished little dolls, dressed in panel-picked preppy clothes and painted in "natural" makeup. There's a bow in Dusk's hair. We look nothing like ourselves. I take solace in that. This is not us.

I wish Daphne had been right that this scandal could have bankrupted GreenGrove. It would make me happier to see the company in ashes, bankrupt after compensating the businesses they destroyed. But the start-up was more firmly rooted than we knew.

They have the resources to make up for what they've done—at least financially. Which means they never needed the Harvest Host in the first place. They ruined my life on the off chance it would save them a slight dip in profits.

Mackey's speech finally ends, and I step off the stage to find a water fountain. They gave us a short tour of city hall before the press conference began, but it's a big building and I find myself in a dead-end corridor. As I turn to retrace my steps, I hear voices, and tuck myself behind an avant-garde block statue.

"I think that went well," I hear Mackey say.

"I agree," replies a voice I have a face but no name for, one of the many city officials involved in the logistics of this little play we put on today.

"I told you this would blow over," Mackey continues. "The settlements with the businesses are simple matters with our lawyers, and the positive press from paying those little girls cleans up any social mishaps."

"The numbers are looking good," the official admits. "We'll likely be able to reopen negotiations on the citywide contract in a week. Maybe two."

"My man, Johnson!" Mackey says. "I've got a meeting, so I gotta jet, but I'll touch base with you Monday. Sound good?"

I don't hear Johnson's reply, but he must respond positively because the CEO laughs. I look out from behind the statue to see them both walking back the way they came and then splitting up. Johnson heads back in the direction of the reporters and my friends. Jeremy Mackey goes in the opposite direction.

I can't believe it. Not only is GreenGrove going to survive this scandal, but the city is still going to give them the contract?

My renewed anger spurs me to follow Mackey to the parking lot, where a fancy convertible sports car unlocks at a press of the key fob in his hand. The afternoon is fading, as is my chance for justice.

"None of this means anything to you, does it?" I ask him. My voice is dripping with disgust, but my clear hatred doesn't even make him flinch.

Mackey chuckles. He opens the car door and leans inside, pressing a button that retracts the top. "Hey there, sweetheart," he says jovially, like a too-familiar extended relative at a family reunion. "Thanks for coming today."

"You can't fix everything with money."

"The thing is," he says, "you really can. I'm sorry you got mixed up in all this, but I'm sure you'll find that that check helps." He loosens his tie and tosses it in the back seat. "I'll tell you a secret," he adds in a stage whisper. "We called it a scholarship, but legally it's not classified as one. The funds aren't locked to educational spending, so feel free to go wild. I won't tell anyone."

I walk toward him, the heels of the ribbon sandals they sent with this dress tapping the pavement aggressively with each step. "What's to stop you from doing this again?"

His jaw clenches and I see the exact moment he realizes that I was just playing a part today. The demure little girl he thought he was talking to is an illusion. Originally, I was the perfect monster for his misdoings. I've bested his plans for me once already. He can't control me outside of the conference.

"Kid—" he says.

"Don't talk to me like you know me!" I snap. Suddenly, the volume on his car stereo kicks on at full volume, to a deafening screech. He leans over the driver's side door to silence it, but an alarm goes off instead and the headlights begin flashing.

Mackey ignores me as he mashes buttons to try to quiet his car, but technology doesn't seem to be his friend anymore. He's fully distracted now and I know I've lost his attention. I don't matter, and nothing I say will make a difference.

I decide to leave him to his ego-induced mayhem and turn to reenter city hall. As I do, a woman I didn't hear approaching passes right by me. I shiver at an unexpected cold breeze, but it doesn't seem to bother her. She wears a flowing long-sleeved blouse with an ascot and a long button-down skirt. I smile at her as she walks away, joking, "You wear that ascot a lot better than my friend Fred does." She doesn't turn to look at me. I guess not even this preppy getup is enough to make me acceptable.

I attempt to brush it off and continue on, but I stop

when I hear the CEO complaining yet again. I spin around, hoping that Ascot Lady is chewing him out for parking in her assigned spot or something. But what I see instead is so confusing I start walking back toward the car, just to make sure my eyes aren't lying to me.

The chaotic symphony of malfunctioning electronics has stopped. In its place, the woman has invaded Mackey's car. She's sitting in the passenger seat. He's in the driver's seat, hands on the wheel, and seems very unhappy with his new guest. "I told you to get out!" he yells at her. She grabs him by both arms and makes her own demand.

"Leave Coolsville," she says coldly. Her voice is rough and loud, like metal being dragged across concrete.

"No!" he yells. She lets go of one arm but maintains her white-knuckle grip on the other, and he shudders. "No!" he cries out again, but it's like he's yelling at himself instead of her. "Stop it!"

The car suddenly accelerates, heading directly at the building. Directly toward *me*. Startled, I jump out of the way just in time, rolling hard on the sunbaked cement. I hear the crash before I see it. Sucking in a gasp at the pain blossoming on my scraped cheek, I blink through eyelashes brushed with gravel and blood dripping from a cut on my forehead.

The flashy vehicle is crumpled flat as a pancake against the brick exterior of city hall. Blood flows down Jeremy Mackey's hanging arm, the only part of him visible in the wreckage. It drips off his luxury watch. On his sleeve, where the woman was holding him, is a smear of bright gold dust.

I look at the passenger seat and gasp. It's empty. The woman somehow stands outside the mangled car. Untouched.

My fingers scramble for purchase on the gravel as I try to crawl away. But I have to understand. "How did you get out?" I ask, but I fear I already know.

The woman shifts her attention to me. There's something off about her eyes. They're too bright. Too gold, like the sun is reflected in her gaze. They fade to black as she focuses them on me. "You," she says. "You're ruining my town too." She starts walking straight toward me, despite the wreckage between us.

When she reaches the car, she doesn't pause. She walks *through* it. The brightness of her eyes ricochets through her body, turning her veins solid gold. I scurry back farther, feeling rocks cut up my palms, but before I can scream someone else does.

I look behind me. The noise of the crash has attracted a crowd. Dozens of office workers are rushing to the scene of the accident. "Stop!" I yell, trying to warn them. "She—"

I start, turning back toward the woman.

"She," I repeat. I look everywhere until the dribbles of blood above my eyes coagulate into a slow-moving waterfall. "She's gone."

CHAPTER TWENTY-SEVEN

It's not over. It's not over. It's not over.

That's all I can think as I lie to Fred's father while he interrogates me at yet another crime scene. I can't tell him about the woman with the gold eyes. He won't believe me. And even if he did, this town won't do anything about her, because they won't face it. They can't stop her.

There's only one group that can.

"I think it was a tech issue," I tell the sheriff. "His lights and stereo were going berserk right before it happened. I've read stories about self-driving cars malfunctioning. I don't know if his was one of those, but maybe?"

"That's certainly possible," Sheriff Jones says. "I'm sorry you had to witness something so awful, Ms. McKnight." I rub my thumb across the bandage the paramedics put above my eyebrows, at a loss for how to respond to the sheriff when he treats me like an actual victim instead of a suspect. The Coolsville Police Department is so much easier to deal with when you give them the simplest possible answer.

Even if it's nowhere close to the truth.

I know I won't find my friends anywhere near the crime scene, so I text the group chat when I'm dismissed and have them pick me up in the Mystery Machine two blocks away.

Fred starts driving before I've even fully closed the door. With Luna and Dusk joining the gang again, the van is so packed even without Velma that there's barely room to breathe. No one asks me any questions until we stop at a dog park that's empty, having technically closed to the public at six.

"We heard there was a car accident," Luna says. She takes the barrettes out of her hair as she speaks, freeing her hair back into its natural 'fro.

"And that someone died," Daphne whispers. She's pale at the thought. Scooby puts his head on her knees, rubbing until she acquiesces to petting him.

"But in the parking lot?" Dusk questions. "I don't understand how more than a fender bender could happen there."

"It was the CEO of GreenGrove," I say. "He crashed his car into the side of the building. I led Sheriff Jones to think it could have been a freak accident, but I saw it all. He drove himself into that wall. But he wasn't alone."

"Someone else was in the car with him?" Shaggy asks.

"Not some*one*," I correct. "Some*thing*."

Scooby whimpers as I tell them about the woman with the ascot. I don't blame him. It's an unbelievable story, but I can tell they don't doubt me. The first comment after my retelling is comical when Daphne points out, "No one wears ascots but Fred."

"That's what I said!" I laugh, relieved I'm still capable of being amused after seeing two dead bodies in less than a week. "I told her she wore it better than he does, but she ignored me. At least until after the murder."

"Instead of mocking my fashion sense *again*," Fred interjects, "could we focus on the facts?"

"She said you were ruining her town," Luna states.

"Told the CEO to leave Coolsville too," Shaggy says, sitting cross-legged on the grass. Scooby rests his head in his lap. "Maybe we should take the advice he didn't and get out of Dodge."

"We can't," Daphne says. "Not without Velma."

She tugs at Fred's sleeve. He sighs. "You said she was wearing a long-sleeved blouse and a button-down skirt," he says. "That's not as rare as my ascot, but all together it sounds like pretty typical pioneer wear. I think this Gold Ghost is Laura Coolidge."

The rest of Mystery Inc. doesn't seem nearly as shocked by this as Dusk, Luna, and I are. The only one among them whose expression changes from resigned frustration is Shaggy, who tilts his head back and groans.

"Another angry ghost?" Luna asks.

"Velma was looking into her as a possibility if the GreenGrove theory didn't pan out," Fred says, "but once most of the evidence started pointing toward plain old corporate corruption she set it aside."

"Why would she be haunting Coolsville?" Dusk asks. "Isn't she one of the founders? She should love this place. Why would she want to harm anyone here?"

I feel so foolish for not recognizing Laura Coolidge immediately. She looks exactly as she did in her portrait in the school library. Her eyes glowed such a vicious gold. The same color as her handprint on Jeremy Mackey's lifeless arm.

"Oh no," I whisper as another memory surfaces. All attention turns to me. "She left a gold residue on GreenGrove's CEO where she grabbed him. At the school, when we discovered Jordan's body, her hand was covered in gold. I thought it was metallic spray paint from where she was tagging the greenhouse."

"That fits with the theory Velma was looking into," Fred says. "She didn't think Laura was trying to hurt the town. She thought that, in Laura's mind, she was protecting it."

"By killing people," Luna points out.

"On my first day of school, I tried to help a boy who

split his bag on the base of Laura's statue in the campus courtyard," I admit. "He was so rude about it. I got angry and began to confront him, when the statue toppled after there was this weird metallic fog. It left behind a smear of dust then, too. I thought it was just residue from the statue. I didn't tell anybody about it because I was worried it was my magic that caused it."

"You've never hurt anyone with your magic, though," Dusk says. "Not even accidentally."

"If Laura thought the boy was vandalizing her monument, she could have tried to stop him," Daphne says. "Maybe all the damage from GreenGrove's scheme made her more powerful, more vindictive. I don't know." She sighs. "It's just a theory without more information on her past. What upset her. What motivated her, in life and in death."

"Velma asked to borrow my book on Coolsville and Crystal Cove," I say. "She had questions about the Ruby wagon train. There were a lot of tragedies on the journey to founding the town. I thought she was just curious."

Serenity is the only solution for Coolsville.

"She probably still has some of her research with her," Shaggy says. "Which means it'll be at the hospital."

Fred spins his keys on one finger. "Then we better get going."

We screech into the hospital parking garage just before visiting hours end for the day. The nurse at the help desk is not charmed by the size of our group, which we considered on the drive over. Shaggy talks around the truth to try to convince her Scooby is a service dog. Dusk stays with the two of them as backup. The rest of us head for Velma's room.

"Velma's friends?" a cheerier nurse says with a smile. Her grin matches the carefree joy of the illustrated kittens on her scrubs. "I recognized your bright red streaks," she says to me. "What a treat! She'll be happy to see you."

"She's awake?" I ask.

"She might be resting now, but she woke a few hours ago," the cartoon cat nurse says. "I asked her if she wanted me to call anyone, but she saw on the TV that you were all busy at some event and told me she'd just study until you were done. Never seen a patient willing do homework in the hospital. She's an interesting one, your friend."

Daphne thanks the nurse. I hear her attempts to cut the chatterbox off as I stride down the hall. I don't have any more niceties in me today. Besides, we have a town to save—again—and the longer I'm left alone with my memories, the more puzzle pieces slot together.

The gold dust on Jeremy Mackey's sleeve was the exact same shade as what I thought was paint on Jordan's hand *and* on the place where the light broke off during talent show rehearsals. Then I remember, today wasn't the first time I saw someone other than Fred wearing an ascot. I thought it was him in the hall the night we broke into school. There was the figure in the shadows, the unnatural source behind the flickering lights that forced me to attempt the banishing spell a day early. Flickering lights . . . just like Mackey's car before he drove it into the wall.

It was Laura Coolidge who let the stage light loose and tried to hit me with it. It was also Laura in the school hall that night telling me to leave. She's been coming after me the whole time.

And she killed Jeremy and Jordan. Because in her eyes they harmed the reputation of Coolsville. Vandalism. Property destruction. Apparently, the punishment for those is death, according to her.

But I have hope, because I sent her away once. Banished her temporarily that night at school, with the spell I was practicing for the pumpkin patch. It never would have worked on the Harvest Host, because the mist monster was just an illusion. It was a soulless creation of greedy tech. It had no connection to the earth. I had no power over it.

I know my power now, but what if it's too late?

Velma's room is empty when I enter it. The television is still on, on a local news channel that's covering Jeremy Mackey's untimely death instead of his triumph at the press conference. There are books strewn across the bed. A journal lies open in the center of them.

"Is she in the bathroom?" Luna asks as she, Fred, and Daphne enter the room.

I ignore them and take a look at Velma's books. Velma's pile shows she came to the same conclusion as the rest of us, all on her own. She has tons of evidence: handwritten notes from various books and dozens of newspaper clippings ranging from a string of break-ins that ended suddenly and without a culprit caught to a few freak "accidents" similar to Jordan's fall from the greenhouse roof onto the spikes of the trellis.

Based on the dates in Velma's journal, she's been looking into Laura Coolidge's crimes for a long time. Since before I even came to Coolsville.

"She's not here," Fred concludes after checking the bathroom attached to the room. I haven't moved from where I stand next to her book-covered bed.

"Velma knew Laura would come for me," I say, "even though you proved my innocence. Intentions don't matter to Laura. She was never going to leave me alone." I trace letters of Velma's light script. She writes like her pen is a feather, light enough to race across the page to keep up with her racing brain. "'I am now of the opinion that the Ruby train didn't fall from natural causes,'" I read aloud from our friend's journal. "'I believe that Laura Ruby took a preventative approach to trouble. She eliminated anything or anyone she felt threatened the future she wanted for her family.'"

"Thorn," Daphne says softly, cautiously, "there's something I think you should see."

"The gold dust," I confirm, not looking up from Velma's notes. "On the floor under the bed. On the edge of the sheets." I run my hand across the stationery again. "On the

224

page of the open book near her pillow. I know. I saw it the moment I came into the room."

"Did Laura take her?" Luna asks.

"No," I say. "I think Velma went willingly."

I move the books and show them the map Velma and I used to plan the museum trip, now spread out on the bedspread. She was using her books to keep the edges from curling up, just like she did at the library. The day she surprised me with the gummy bears. The day Jordan died.

But Velma has made some new additions to the map since I last saw it. In the sections she highlighted to track the host, she's marked different spots in black ink. Next to the marks, in large print below the conclusion I just shared with the gang, she wrote: She's drawn to what belonged to her.

Almost every building of importance in the town is crossed out with a black X, except the museum. That, Velma has simply labeled the Coolidge exhibit.

"And she's told us exactly where to find her," I say.

I step away from the bed while the others take in what I've found. "Okay," Fred says, "but we don't go in without a plan."

"I agree," I say. "And I've got the start of one. But we need to stop by my place first. I'm done with these country club heels, anyway. I need my boots to kick Laura Coolidge back to hell."

CHAPTER TWENTY-EIGHT

Daphne doesn't have a key to the museum, even with a wing dedicated to her family, but it turns out she's good at picking locks, too. There's no janitorial staff to avoid this time. The museum has yet to reopen, despite being released as a crime scene a few days ago. We discovered Velma missing only half an hour ago, but every second without securing her safety feels like ages.

I tap my foot—heavy with the heft of my tallest, blackest boots—on the polished marble floor. I'm nowhere near the

Coolidge exhibit, but I have to play my part if the plan is going to work. It has to work. There's no other option.

I've defeated an undead witch before. I can do it again.

I shake the can of spray paint in my hand. "Laura!" I call as I spray a blood-red trail of paint across a display case. "I know what you did to your first community. I know what you've sacrificed for Coolsville. *Who* you've sacrificed." I spray the paint in an arc across another glass case.

I'd read more of Velma's findings aloud to the gang as we drove here. She theorized that Laura Coolidge could only manifest near items she once owned. That explained why not every misguided delinquent in Coolsville met a bloody end. The Coolidges are memorialized at most important buildings in town, with property deeds and small possessions on display at city hall, the high school, even the post office.

But none of those locations hold as many artifacts as the museum.

"It's me you want," I remind her. "You know the truth. I am Thorn McKnight, descendant of Ravencroft blood. One town is already left in ashes in my wake. I bet Velma wanted you to spare me. But you know better than that. That's why you took her, right?"

You were right, Jordan, I think as I repeat her final actions. Paint from the can drips down my wrist, like blood from this internal wound. *I wish you were here to hate me for it.*

"You don't belong in Coolsville!" Laura screeches as she

appears, flickering into form. Her rage twists her beautiful face into a terrifying mask. Her veins flow with liquid gold; glowing trails bleed from her sunbeam eyes.

I flip the can of paint in my hand, then flee down a nearby corridor. "The gold rush is alight!" I yell as I slide under a table at a four-pronged intersection. Stationed at the other three paths are Fred, Daphne, and Shaggy. They each hold a can of the same spray paint, part of our plan to summon Laura by defiling the biggest collection of Coolsville artifacts in town.

"You meddling kids," Laura snarls at the gang. She hovers above us. The lights of the displays pulse on and off with her fury. "You should know better. You should honor your town, not desecrate it."

"I think we can do both," Shaggy says. The three of them take off down their respective corridors. Laura goes after Shaggy first. I fight the urge to help; I have to stay on task. I run back the way I came.

"Leave him alone!" Daphne yells. I look back without stopping to see the trio crisscrossing between their halls, leading Laura in gold-dusted circles. They laugh as if this life-and-death situation is the most fun they've had in a while.

I reach the third milestone, the T. rex skull. "Scooby?" I ask softly. I can't see him in the dim light, but I feel him rubbing up against my midsection. "There you are," I say, taking his head in both my hands and bending to kiss his forehead. "Take me to the Hex Girls."

He runs, faster than me, but I follow the slapping of his paws to the Blake wing. I can picture the wing vividly, even in the dark. I remember it from our final sting. This is where I gave Velma an out on the complication of us. *I know what I want,* she said to me.

Her words were vague, but her actions have been anything but. Her feelings for me aren't cryptic or unproved. There is hard evidence to us. Our relationship is new, but solid. Given every opportunity to abandon me, she's chosen to do the opposite, even when it put her at risk.

The Coolidge exhibit should be at the end of this hall, just after the entrance to the wing. Scooby trots to a large globe near the wall and then past it. "Good boy," Dusk's voice says. I follow Scooby and see my best friends stand up from their hiding spot.

"Do you have it?" I ask. Luna nods, holding up the backpack I stuffed with supplies at my house.

We tiptoe down the hall and into the room with the Coolidge exhibit. It's decorated in a different manner from the rest of the stark white modern museum. It's like stepping into Levi and Laura's home. Everything is wood paneled, the matching tables artfully distressed. The artifact cases break the illusion, with the same locked glass boxes as the rest of the building bolted to the wood walls and surfaces. It's instantly clear why Velma circled this as the place to find her.

This is what binds Laura to Coolsville. I would have felt it when we came here the first time, if I had gotten this far.

Her energy is all over the room, just as dark and demanding as Sarah Ravencroft and her spell book that fateful night in Oakhaven. But a stronger presence calls to me. I step deeper into the room, squinting until my eyes adjust to the darker surroundings. Scooby moves with me, as if he can sense her too.

There, seated at one of the wood tables, is Velma.

CHAPTER TWENTY-NINE

Velma is covered in significantly more gold dust than either of Laura's previous victims. It's all over her ankles, her shoulders, her hands, which are folded atop each other in a pose of perfect decorum. She sits with flawless posture, her eyes closed.

Statue still.

I swallow my fear. "Like I showed you," I instruct Luna and Dusk. They drop to the floor and start unloading the backpack. As they perform their task, I inch toward Velma.

It's hard to stay quiet on the creaking hardwood floor, but she doesn't acknowledge our presence. She doesn't move as I approach. *Why did you risk yourself for me?* I scream at her silently. The gold dust kisses her soft features, settling over every curve and crease. My hands shake uncontrollably as they hover above her own. I don't want to touch her. I don't want to know.

I won't be able to take it if . . . But I have to face the truth.

I touch her folded hands.

She gasps. Her eyes start open, kicking a small shimmer of metallic from her lashes. She smiles at me and juts her chin forward as if to kiss me, but she can't seem to move the rest of her body. She's not in control of it, just like the GreenGrove CEO in his car.

"The dust," Velma says. "I'm stuck."

"Why hasn't she killed you yet?" I ask.

"I called her to me with a piece of rubble from her statue at the school that I've been carrying with me. I convinced her that she had changed my mind. That I believed in her mission to protect Coolsville," Velma says. "I knew you guys would figure it out. I knew you'd come after me."

"You summoned her?" I ask, dumbfounded. "No. You led her into a trap."

Velma's dust-locked shoulders twitch up slightly in what I assume was meant to be a casual shrug. "It's what we do," she says. "I bought you all a bit more time. It's not a big deal."

I want to kiss her stupid, self-sacrificing face. I think I

could suck the selflessness out through her tongue, if I tried hard enough. I'm going to do it. After this is over, I'm going to make out with her for so long that the oxygen loss brings her IQ back down to those of us normal mortals. I'll have her so distracted she forgets about monsters entirely.

"Thorn!" Dusk calls from behind me.

I twist my head, my palm still on Velma's folded hands. We have visitors.

A paint-splattered Shaggy slides into the room, quickly followed by Daphne and Fred. Scooby keeps guarding Velma. He raises his hackles, a low, constant warning rumbling from his throat. "She's right behind us!" Shaggy yells, scrambling across the floor on hands and knees.

"Careful!" Luna calls, repairing her work where he smudged it.

I look back to Velma. "Stay put," I say without thinking, then wince. "Sorry." She's merciful enough not to roll her eyes at me. I squeeze her hand before letting go.

I ache with the loss of her touch, my fingers spasming like overworked muscles, but everyone else has stuck to the script. The gold dust has transferred to my hand, branding me, but I don't care. I make my way to my mark. It's time for the star of the show. I pull my mother's journal from my now-empty backpack on the ground.

Laura's glow enters the room before she does. I can't help squinting at the brightness. It takes effort not to cower from the light, but I stand my ground. I adopt my stage voice to be heard over the crackling of her angry-lightning veins.

"We're not so different," I tell her. "Since I moved here, all I've wanted was to fit into your town. I liked the idea of serenity, but I didn't understand the cost. I didn't realize how many people could be hurt in the quest to pretend life is always perfect. Coolsville is *not* perfect, despite everything you've done. You've made me realize that if I'm always running in fear of the darkness of my past, I'll never have time to enjoy the light."

Even if it's blinding right now.

I blink rapidly to adjust to her brightness as she laughs at me. "You are nothing like me, child," she says. "You are too dark, too garish, too abnormal for my Coolsville." She dims slightly as she talks, from a suffocating glow to a steady one.

I nod, using the moment to subtly monitor the gang at my feet. "That's fine," I say. "I like myself better that way." I tilt my head back until I'm eye to eye with her again.

"Now!" I yell.

Another light, separate from Laura's unnatural illumination, fills the room. Laura looks down, screeching in anger when she realizes the source of the second glow. The two of us are at the center of a large Wiccan pentagram drawn in chalk on the floor of the precious re-creation of her former home. My friends sit at each point of the star-shaped sigil, a lit candle in front of them all.

I open my mother's journal and begin to recite the revised version I wrote of her banishment spell. "Laura Coolidge, your presence is no longer necessary in Coolsville. Your protection is no longer wanted. You are not welcome here. I banish you by the powers of the Goddess and God. I banish you by the powers of the Sun, Moon, and Stars—"

Laura knocks my mother's journal from my hands. She closes her skeletal hands around my wrists, marring the sleeves of my black jacket with two garish gold handprint. I'm surprised that despite the warmth of her golden eyes, she's actually quite cold, feeling it deep in my bones where she grabbed me. The bite of her hold creeps through the fabric and up my arms.

"I won't let some foreign interloper destroy the town I gave up everything to build," she hisses in my face.

"I'm from the East Coast, not another country," I say. "Take a cue from the billboards and chill out."

I look down to make sure my mother's journal didn't fall onto any of the lit candles. Laura follows my gaze, grinning wickedly when I look back up at her. Velma was right. The power of Laura's hold is immobilizing. I can't bend to retrieve the journal. But that's fine.

I keep my palms facing up, gesturing skyward to the east and west points of the pentagram, as they were when Laura grabbed me. "I don't need it," I tell her. "I know what I need to do. I know who I am now. I banish you by the powers of the Earth."

Luna, stationed at the bottom left of the pentagram, shakes soil from a jar along the line of chalk closest to her.

"I banish you by the powers of Water."

Shaggy fills a chalice with water.

"I banish you by the powers of Fire."

Fred lights a match and drops it in a bowl filled with paper scraps.

"I banish you by the powers of Air."

Daphne lights a bundle of incense with the candle at her point of the pentagram and waves the smoke along the line leading to her.

Laura growls, but she's weakening. Her glow is fading. I stay where I am, even though her hold on me has slackened. She can't keep me anymore.

But I'm not done.

"This is no longer your town to protect," I inform her. "It's mine."

"And mine," Dusk repeats at the head of the pentagram, the spot of the spirit. As each of my friends repeats the mantra at their stations on the star, claiming Coolsville for themselves, Laura tries to leave the pentagram, but an invisible force now holds her here with me.

"You'll change everything!" she screeches as she flickers like a dying light bulb.

"Maybe that's for the best," I say, holding tight to the power thrumming through my veins as hers fades before me.

Laura shakes her head. "I can't!" she cries, less vitriolic but still commanding in the small space. "I can't lose it all again."

"You created a beautiful town," I admit, "but we can't live in the past forever. We have to move on. And so do you." She pauses for a moment, and her face morphs from enraged to curious, as if she's pondering the concept of something after this.

And finally, she releases me, disintegrating in a bright, golden flash.

Scooby barks, jumping into the pentagram and biting at the residual glitter. Luna presses on his paws, trying to keep him from stepping on any of the candles until they've all been blown out.

After the air clears, all that's left of Laura Coolidge is a single gold nugget. I crouch to pick it up and drop it in the pocket of the jacket she ruined. I'll hold on to it until I find somewhere safer to put it. I'll have to do more research to make sure we've bound Laura tight enough to prevent her ever escaping again, but it will do for now.

When I stand up, I nearly fall over with the weight of Velma rushing me. "You did it!" she says, burying her golden hands in my hair and pressing herself heart to heart against me. My jacket is surely done for now, but so is the press conference dress. Silver linings, I guess.

She allows only enough space between us to rest her hands on the back of my neck. Her smiling lips are the only thing in my sight as I watch them say, "I knew you could. You're the bravest person I know."

And then Velma kisses me. In front of everyone.

One of her hands relinquishes my neck to return to my hair, dragging me down to her height. I go willingly. I'd go anywhere for her, but it's here—right now, this moment— that I know I'll find myself returning to until the end of time. Safe. Alive. Surrounded, by choice. She's chosen me in front of the only people who matter.

I'm hers.

When we part, panting, I search her face for any regret or embarrassment at what she's done, but there's nothing but joy. Together we look around at the gang, Luna, and Dusk. No one voices any surprise or shock. They're all simply happy.

And tired.

"Finally," Dusk says, voice teasingly long-suffering. "But if you think that's gonna keep you from helping us clean up the museum before sunrise, I promise you won't live to hard launch at next year's Pride parade."

CHAPTER THIRTY

SIX WEEKS LATER...

I peek through the curtain, seeking Velma's red headband in the front row of the auditorium once again. It's the night of the rescheduled talent show, but she's been distracting me from the acts. She wore red to match me tonight.

"Stop!" Luna whisper-yells, dragging me away from the front of the stage. "You're gonna miss our cue."

"I promise I won't," I tell her, even though my head is already turning back in the direction of the velvet headband.

"Check my makeup," Luna says. I erase my girlfriend from my focus best as I can, knowing Luna will kill me if I let her go out there with smeared lip liner.

"Smile," I command, baring my own teeth as an example. She flashes me a big smile. No lipstick specks. "You're perfect."

Her eyes crease under purple shadow the same shade as her nails. She shakes her hands out in a pantomime of nervous jazz hands and starts yet another vocal warm-up. I join her simply to make her look less insane. Luna is the most reasonable member of our band, except on performance days.

"They completely sold out!" Dusk announces when she finds us again. That was the last thing that set Luna off, Dusk ducking out ahead of the act before ours to check the ticket sales. But Luna doesn't rant at her about it, because even in her pre-gig anxiety she understands why.

The proceeds from tonight's show are being put toward rehabilitating the soil and planting a new batch of crops to replace the ones killed by GreenGrove. We donated our entire check from them to the cause, but the legal battles that a lot of the affected businesses brought against the company after the press conference are slow going, and many of them were relying on their fall bounty to keep afloat.

That's still the biggest scandal on the minds of Coolsville residents. The town remains as blissfully unaware of the dispatchment of Laura Coolidge as they were of her "protection," but we can see the signs everywhere. The group chat comes alive daily with gossip about the latest break in *serenity*, even if it's something as small as a yard ornament war between neighbors. The longer Laura is gone, the less serene—and more interesting—Coolsville is sure to become.

It feels weird that the talent show Jordan died trying to keep me out of is now raising money to fix the garden where she died, but I guess a town so used to sweeping its few bad events under the rug isn't well-versed yet in the proper decorum post ghost-murder of a resident. Postponing the show a month was the best they could do.

I'm not sure how I fit in the New Coolsville yet either. It's still brighter and more colorful than I'd prefer, but I can't deny I like the locals. Some a tiny bit more than others.

My favorite locals are definitely enjoying the disruption to the status quo.

I'm happy to finally focus on my music again. I only look at Velma twice as we walk out to greet the audience, and I also give my dad, who is sitting next to her, a smile. I can't wait to hear their thoughts on our change of song choice. The gang heard the old version back in Oakhaven, but I've never felt more connected to the lyrics than I do now. I know it's the right choice for this show.

I smile at the crowd from the microphone, counting the drumbeat Dusk begins behind me. Luna joins in, and then I sing the first line of the opening chorus of our song "Earth, Water, Fire, and Air," repeating the elements that helped us stop Laura's reign of terror in Coolsville.

I strum the guitar into the first verse. We haven't sung this song since the night after the Ravencrofts burned Oakhaven. Writer's block followed me when we moved, tainting my pen with the same fear that kept me from Wicca. I'm no longer afraid of magic or melody, but the latest lyrics to have inspired me are still in the early stages of songwriting.

It doesn't bother me to rehash an old favorite as I see my friends and father rise from their seats to sing along with the chorus when we hit it out again. I spin on the stage and try to stop my growing smile from changing my pitch. I know I have time now. I have space to experiment with my music, my interests, and everything that our new home can teach me.

I croon to the crowd, then turn to look only at my best friends as we unite on the closing chorus. The spirit is infectious and a bigger part of the audience sings along.

I hold the final note as long as I can as the girls come up behind me. We close out with a killer strum to wild applause, but I don't even look back at the crowd as we walk off the stage.

I don't really care what the town thinks of me anymore. I won't even be too broken up if we don't win tonight. Reunited with my best friends, hugging them backstage as the next act takes our place, I feel like I've already won.

"We did awesome," Dusk squeals.

"I knew we would," Luna says. We all burst into laughter at that. "I'm serious," she insists through poor attempts at a straight face. "Whatever. Thorn, did you bring your throat potion for our vocal cords?"

"My herbal vapors?" I ask. "Sure did!" I walk to my backpack, where I left my thermos of peppermint and clove tea. I pull it out and then reach back inside for my phone, planning to text the gang that we'll be out in a few.

My phone buzzes in my hand, several missed messages highlighted on the screen. I click into the group chat.

Velma linked a news article just before the show began. No one has sent any messages since the curtain rose, but the gang chatted a bit right before.

Velma: A suit of armor has gone missing from the museum.

Shaggy: It wasn't us! We were there a month ago.

Daphne: The article says it happened last night.

Fred: It also says it looks like the armor walked out . . . by itself!

I smile as I drop my phone back in my bag and return to the band with my thermos, pouring out a steaming serving to share in the lid that doubles as a cup. I'll leave Mystery Inc. to solve this new case on their own.

I'm no longer terrified of things that go bump in the night, but I'm ready to make my own mark on this town.

I'm not hiding from my past, my bloodline, or even my real name. I know now that, just like my practice in Wicca, who I am is only defined by who I choose to be.

But if the gang needs a little magical assistance . . . well, they know where to find me.

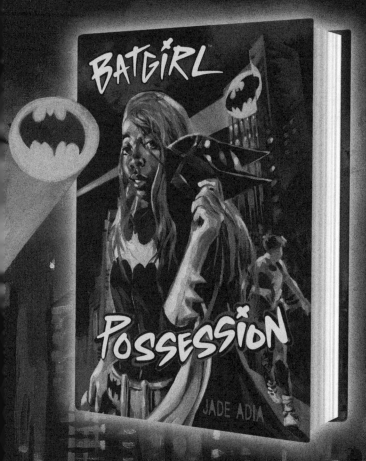